"You're not the kind of [...] with a girl like me."

Caleb couldn't deny the truth. He didn't fool around with good girls, regardless of how well they cooked. "What's your point?"

Pandora's delicate fingers skipped down the row of pearly buttons, unfastening her dress as they went. Caleb had faced strung-out drug dealers shoving guns in his gut and had kept his cool. But the minute the buttons cleared her belly button, he swore the room did a slow spin.

Damn, she was incredible.

She walked toward him, the black dress hanging loose from her shoulders. When she reached him, Caleb's hand automatically gripped her hips. She smiled, then leaned even closer so her body pressed tight against his. She reached between them and slid her palm over the hard length of his sex, making his erection jump desperately against the constraining fabric of his slacks.

He groaned in delight.

"And that's the proof that the aphrodisiacs work," Pandora told him just before she pressed her mouth to his.

Blaze™

Dear Reader,

Do you believe in aphrodisiacs? I love the idea that something delicious can have a little extra punch (especially during the holidays, when there are so many yummy things around!) And when I had two reluctant characters who needed a nudge in the right direction, what else could I do but offer them something irresistible to push them over the sensual edge. In this case, that something included chocolate.

Sex, Lies and Mistletoe features two very special guests: Paulie and Bonnie, cats who live at the Furry Friends Animal Shelter. Find out about them, and all the other Blaze Authors' Pet Project pets, on the Blaze Authors' blog—http://blazeauthors.com. Please come by and say hi!

And if you're on the web, be sure to drop by my website at www.tawnyweber.com. While you're there, check out my members-only section with its special contests, excerpts and other fun.

Happy holidays!

Tawny Weber

Tawny Weber

SEX, LIES AND MISTLETOE

TORONTO NEW YORK LONDON
AMSTERDAM PARIS SYDNEY HAMBURG
STOCKHOLM ATHENS TOKYO MILAN MADRID
PRAGUE WARSAW BUDAPEST AUCKLAND

Recycling programs
for this product may
not exist in your area.

ISBN-13: 978-0-373-79660-1

SEX, LIES AND MISTLETOE

Copyright © 2011 by Tawny Weber

www.Harlequin.com

Printed in U.S.A.

ABOUT THE AUTHOR

Tawny Weber is usually found dreaming up stories in her California home, surrounded by dogs, cats and kids. When she's not writing hot, spicy stories for Harlequin Blaze, she's shopping for the perfect pair of shoes or scrapbooking happy memories. Come by and visit her on the web at www.tawnyweber.com or on Facebook at www.facebook.com/TawnyWeber.RomanceAuthor.

Books by Tawny Weber

To all the wonderful people who read my books.
You bring untold joy to my life. Thank you!

Prologue

"I've made the arrangements. Everything is in place."

As the assurance echoed through his speakerphone, Tobias Black leaned back in his Barcalounger, shifted an unlit cigar between his teeth and grinned.

"That was fast. I didn't think you'd pull it off."

A lie, of course.

He'd known once the challenge was issued, it'd be impossible to resist. Just as he'd known that the person he'd challenged had the power to make it happen. Tobias Black only worked with the best. Even when the best's main goal in life had once been to arrest him.

Tobias looked at the pictures framed and fading on his study wall. A gap-toothed trio of schoolkids with wicked looks in their golden eyes and hair as black as night.

Damn, he missed them. All three had turned their backs on him eight years ago. Caleb because he rejected what his father stood for. Maya out of disappointment. And Gabriel? Tobias gave the photo of his middle child, his youngest son, a worried frown. Gabriel in fury, determined to prove that he was twice as good and twice as clever as his old man.

They'd all felt justified in leaving.

And Tobias felt justified in bringing them back. A man

spent his life building a legacy, he needed his children to hand it down to.

"You're sure you can handle your part?"

Tobias laughed so hard the cigar fell from his lips. Him? Handle a part? That was like asking if the sun was gonna rise in the morning.

"I'll play my part like Stevie Ray Vaughan played guitar."

Silence. Tobias rolled his eyes. Maybe it wasn't so far-fetched to ask if he could handle the part if he could so easily forget who he was talking to. "Let me rephrase that. I'll play my part like Babe Ruth hit the ball."

"If you're not careful, cockiness could be your downfall."

Tobias almost brushed that away like an irritating bug. Then he sighed. Only a stupid man ignored a fair warning.

"There's a fine line between confidence and cockiness. I'll watch my step." He glanced at his eldest son's photo. "Caleb will take the bait. He won't want to come home, but he will. Loyalty is practically his middle name."

"You think he's loyal to you after all these years?"

"To me? Absolutely not." And that hurt like hell, but it was the price Tobias paid for ignoring his kids to feed his own ego. "But he's loyal to Black Oak."

Tobias was gambling everything on Caleb caring about Black Oak. A small town in the foothills of the Santa Cruz Mountains, Black Oak was in many ways the same as when it'd been founded a hundred years ago. A quaint and friendly community.

And now it had a drug problem. Tobias might have no problem skirting the law—or hell, laughing in its face—but he was a man who had zero tolerance for drugs. Especially when those drugs were being dealt in a way that conveniently pointed the finger his way.

It would be smarter to let the locals deal with the drug problem. If the evidence kept pointing at Tobias, they could be more easily…influenced. Because the sad truth was, there were still a few outstanding crimes that Tobias could be arrested for, with the right evidence. And there were hints that whoever was pulling off this drug ring had access to the right evidence. So bringing the feds in was a huge risk.

Someone was framing him. And they had enough dirt to do the job well. And it looked as if they were planning it all here in Black Oak.

That little bit of info he wouldn't share with the feebies.

Because he knew he had to offer up a big enough lure to get the FBI's attention, but not so big that they'd insist on coming in and playing it their way.

He wanted control of this venture.

"This is a huge undertaking, Black. All indications are that the drugs moving into Black Oak are yours. And now you're planning to play your family, who know you well enough to see the game. You're talking about playing a townful of people, many of whom depend on you. And more important, you're going to have to play the FBI, who, as a general rule, want nothing more than to arrest you."

He wanted to point out that he'd played them all, quite successfully, many times before. But bragging was rude. More important, ego was the first nail in the coffin of a good con.

"And your point is?" he asked instead.

"My point is, you're not as young as you once were. And you've been out of the game for a while." There was a pause, then a soft sigh that made Tobias's smile drop away. "You've got a lot on the line. Are you sure you're willing to risk it all? Because if this goes bad, the FBI is going to reel you in and toss your ass in jail for a good long time."

Tobias rolled the cigar between his fingers, staring at the unlit cylinder.

He considered what he'd built here in Black Oak. After a lifetime of running cons, he'd settled down and gone legit five years ago. He'd been quietly making reparations over the years, but paying back a few hundred grand wasn't going to stop the FBI from nabbing him if they had a chance. He could opt out, let someone else take point. The risks were huge.

But then, so were the stakes. And every good con knew, it was the high-stakes games that were worth playing.

"I can handle it."

"And your kids?"

Tobias sighed, pushing to his feet and pretending his bones didn't protest at stretching quickly in the damp winter chill. He tossed the cigar on his desk and strode over to stand before the pictures.

Caleb, Maya and Gabriel.

Smart kids. Good-looking, shrewd and nimble-fingered, even as little punks. Once, they'd thought he'd spun the sun on the tips of his fingers and carried the moon in his back pocket. Once, they'd believed in him. Once, they'd been in his life.

Now? Now he'd settle for one out of three.

"I can handle it," he repeated.

And before this game was through, he'd know who was behind the drugs, who was trying to set him up. Whatever fledgling crime ring was forming would be busted.

If he won, his kids would be a part of his life again.

And if he lost? At long last, his ass would be locked up in the federal pen.

But Tobias Black didn't lose.

1

DAMN SEX. IT RUINED everything.

"I can't believe I'm back in Black Oak." Pandora Easton's murmur was somewhere between a sigh and a groan as she dropped a dusty, musty-smelling box on the floor behind the sales counter.

"No guy, no matter how good in bed, is worth losing your job, your reputation or your self-respect for," she muttered to herself as she looked around Moonspun Dreams. The morning light played through the dance of the dust motes, adding a slightly dingy air to the struggling New Age store.

Sometimes a girl just needed to come home. Especially when she didn't have a choice.

Even if that home was falling apart.

Two months ago, she'd been on top of the world. An up-and-coming pastry chef for a well-known bakery in San Francisco, a gorgeous boyfriend and a strong belief that her life was—*finally*—pretty freaking awesome.

Then, *poof,* everything she'd worked so hard for the last several years was gone. Destroyed. Because she'd fallen for a pretty face, been conned by a smooth line, and worst of all, ruined by a good lay.

Nope. Never again.

Pandora was home now.

Which was *really* just freaking awesome.

With a heavy sigh, she poked one finger at the box she'd rescued from next to a leaking pipe in the back room. It was unlabeled, so she'd have to see what was inside before she could figure out where to put it.

To disguise the musty scent, she lit a stick of prosperity incense. Then Pandora rubbed a speck of dust off a leaf on the braided money tree she'd brought in this morning to decorate the sales counter, and tidied a row of silken soy wax candles with embedded rose petals.

"Not a bad display from a recently fired bakery manager," she commented to Bonnie.

Bonnie just cocked her head to one side, but didn't comment. Since she was one of the two store cats, Pandora hadn't expected much response. Probably a good thing, since the last thing Pandora's ego needed was anyone, human or feline, to point out all the crazy reasons for her thinking returning home to start her life over was going to work.

The cats, like the rest of Moonspun Dreams, were now Pandora's responsibility. She was excited about the felines. But the jury was still out on the quirky New Age store that'd been in Pandora's family for decades. The very store Pandora had wanted to get away from so badly, she'd left town the day after she'd graduated high school.

Before she could settle into a good pout, the bells rang over the front door. Bringing a bright smile and a burst of fresh air, Kathy Andrews hurried in. One hand held a bakery bag, the other a vat-size cup of coffee.

"I'm here to celebrate," Kathy sang out. She stepped over the black puddle of fur that was Paulie the cat sunning himself on the braided carpet, and waltzed across the scarred wooden floor.

"What are we celebrating?"

"That you're back in Black Oak. That you're taking over the family store. Not just for the month your mom is in Sedona for that psychic convention, but for good. And, more important, we need to celebrate the news that your best friend had some really great sex last night."

Pandora exchanged looks with Bonnie. There it was, sex again. But this was Kathy's sex. It wasn't as if that could mess Pandora's life up.

"I'm not so sure having to come home because I failed out there in the big bad world is an excuse to party," Pandora said with a rueful laugh as she took the bakery bag and peeked inside. "Ooh, my favorite. Mrs. Rae's éclairs. I thought she'd retired."

"Mr. Rae's off competing in some pumpkin-carving contest until next Saturday, leaving Mrs. Rae home alone for their anniversary week. Cecilia said her mom dropped off four dozen éclairs this morning with notice that she'd be making pies, too."

One of the joys and irritations about living in a small town was knowing everyone, and everyone knowing your business. In this case, both women knew Mrs. Rae's irritation meant cherry pie by dinner.

"Cecilia seemed surprised when I mentioned I was coming here," Kathy said, not meeting Pandora's eyes as she took back the bag and selected an éclair. "She said she thought Moonspun Dreams was doing so bad, your mom had given up keeping it open on weekends. I know I should have given her a smackdown, but the éclairs smelled too good."

While Kathy dived into her éclair with an enthusiastic moan, Pandora sighed, looking around the store. When she'd been little, her grandmother had stood behind this counter. The store had been filled with herbs and tinctures, all hand-made by Grammy Leda. She'd sold clothes woven by locals with wool from their own sheep, she'd taught classes on composting and lunar gardening, led women's circles and poured her own candles. Grammy had been, Pandora admitted, a total hippie.

Then, when Pandora had been thirteen, Granny Leda had retired to a little cabin up in Humboldt County to raise chinchillas. And it'd been Cassiopeia's turn.

Her mother's intuitive talents, the surge of interest in all things New Age, and her savvy use of the internet had turned a quirky small-town store into a major player in the New Age market. Moonspun Dreams had thrived.

But now that the economy had tanked and New Age had lost its luster, it was almost imploding. Leaving Pandora with the choice of trying to save it. Or letting it fade into oblivion.

"Cecilia was right. Things are really bad," Pandora said. "No point in risking the best éclairs in the Santa Cruz Mountains over the truth."

"And now Moonspun Dreams is yours. Are you going to give up?" Kathy asked quietly, holding out a fingerful of the rich cream for the cat. They both watched Bonnie take a delicate taste while Pandora mulled over the slim choices available.

Her mother had said that she'd run out of ideas. She'd told Pandora before she left to be the keynote speaker at the annual Scenic Psychics conference that the store was hers now. And it was up to her to decide what to do with it.

After sixty years in the family, close up shop and sell the property.

Or fight to keep it going.

Her stomach pitched, but of the two, she knew there was only one she could live with.

"I can't give up. This is all I have, Kath. Not just my heritage, given that Moonspun Dreams has been in the family for four generations. But it's all *I've* got now."

"What are you going to do? And what can I do to help?"

Both questions were typical of Kathy. And both warmed Pandora to the soul, shoving the fears and stress of trying to save a failing business back a bit.

"I don't know. I've been racking my brain, trying to figure something out." Her smile quirked as she gestured to the small table in the corner. Rich rosewood inset with stars and moons, part of the table was covered by a brocade cloth and a handful of vividly painted cards. "I've finally reached the point of desperation."

Kathy's eyes widened. Pandora had sworn off all things metaphysical back in high school, claiming that she didn't have the talent or skill. The reality was that Cassiopeia was so good at it, nothing Pandora did could measure up. And she'd hated knowing she'd never, ever be good enough.

"What'd the reading say?"

"Tarot really isn't my forte," she excused, filling her mouth with the sweet decadence of her éclair.

"Quit stalling. Even if you don't have that psychic edge like your mom, you still know how to read."

That psychic edge. The family gift. Her heritage.

Her failure.

"The cards weren't any help," she dismissed. "The Lovers, Three of Swords, the Tower, Four of Wands and the Seven of Swords."

The éclair halfway to her lips, Kathy scrunched her nose and shrugged. "I don't understand any of that."

"I don't, either." Pandora's shoulders drooped. "I mean, I know what each card means—I was memorizing tarot definitions before I was conjugating verbs. But I don't have a clue how it applies to Moonspun Dreams. It doesn't help me figure out how to save the business."

Yet more proof that she was a failure when it came to the family gift. Handed down from mother to daughter, that little something extra manifested differently in each generation.

Leda, Pandora's grandmother, had prophetic dreams. Cassiopeia's gift was psychic intuition.

And Pandora's? Somewhere around her seventeenth birthday, her mother had decided Pandora's gift was reading people. Sensing their energy, for good or bad. In other words, she'd glommed desperately onto her daughter's skill at reading body language and tried to convince everyone that it was some sort of gift.

Despite popular belief, it hadn't been her mother's overdramatic lifestyle that had sent Pandora scurrying out of Black Oak as soon as she was legally able. It'd been her disappointment that she was just an average person with no special talent. All she'd wanted was to get away. To build a nice normal life for herself. One where she wasn't always judged, always found lacking.

Then she'd had to scurry right back when that nice normal life idea had blown up in her face.

"You're going to figure it out," Kathy said, her words ringing with loyal assurance. "Your mom wouldn't have trusted you with the store if she didn't have faith, too."

"The store is failing. We'll be closing the doors by the end of the year. I don't think it's as much a matter of trusting me as it is figuring I can't make things any worse."

Pandora eyed the last three cream-filled pastries, debating calories versus comfort.

Comfort, and the lure of sugary goodness, won.

"These are so good," she murmured as she bit into the chocolate-drenched creamy goodness.

"They are. Too bad Mrs. Rae only bakes when she's pissed at her husband. Black Oak has a severe sugar shortage now that she's retired." Kathy gave her a long, considering look. "You worked in a bakery for the last few years, right? Maybe you can take over the task of keeping Black Oak supplied with sweet treats. You know, open a bakery or something."

"Wouldn't that be fun," Pandora said with a laugh. Then, because she was starting to feel a little sick after all that sugary goodness, she set the barely eaten éclair on a napkin and slid to her feet. "But I can't. I have to try to make things work. Try to save Moonspun Dreams. Mom was hoping, since I'd managed the bakery the last two years, that maybe I'd see some idea, have some brilliant business input, that might help."

"And you have nothing at all? No ideas?"

Failure weighing down her shoulders, Pandora looked away so Kathy didn't see the tears burning in her eyes. Her gaze fell on the dusty box she'd hauled in earlier.

"We've got a leak in the storeroom," she said, not caring that the subject change was so blatant as to be pathetic. "Most of the stuff stored in that back corner was in plastic bins, so it's probably seasonal decorations or something. But this box was there, too. It's my great-grandma's writing, and from the dust coating the box, it's been there since she moved away."

"Oh, like a treasure chest," Kathy said, stuffing the éclairs back in the bag and clearing a spot on the counter. "Let's see what's in it."

Pandora set the box on the counter and dug her fingernail under one corner of the packing tape. Pulling it loose, she and Kathy both winced at the dust kicking them in the face.

She lifted the flaps. Kathy gave a disappointed murmur even as Pandora herself grinned, barely resisting clapping her dirty hands together.

"It's just books," Kathy said, poking her finger at one.

"My great-grandma Danae's books," Pandora corrected, pulling out one of the fragile-looking journals. She reverently opened the pages of the velvet-covered book, the handmade paper thick and soft beneath her fingers. "This is better than a treasure chest."

"Oh, sure. Piles of gold coins, glistening jewels and price-

less gems is exactly the same thing as a box of moldy old
books." Still, Kathy reached in and pulled a leather-bound
journal out for herself, flipping through the fragile pages.
Quickly at first, then slower, as the words caught her attention.

"These are spells. Like, magic," she exclaimed, her voice
squeaking with excitement. "Oh, man, this is so cool."

A little giddy herself, Pandora looked over at the book
Kathy was flipping through. "Grammy Danae collected them.
I remember when I was little, before she died, people used
to call her a wisewoman. Grammy Leda said that meant she
was a witch. Mom said she was just a very special lady."

"Do you think she really was a witch?" Kathy asked, glee
and skepticism both shining in her eyes.

"I'm more inclined to believe she was one of the old wives
all those tales were made from." Pandora laughed. "Despite
the rumors, there's nothing weird or freaky about my family."

She wanted—desperately needed—to believe that.

"But wouldn't it be cool if these spells worked? Say, the
love ones. You could sell them, save the store."

"It's not the recipe that makes a great cook, it's the power,"
Pandora recited automatically. At her friend's baffled look,
she shrugged. "That's what Grammy always said. That words,
spells, a bunch of information…that wasn't what made things
happen. Just like the tarot cards don't tell the future, crystals
don't do the healing. It's the intuition, the power, that make
things happen."

"I'll bet people would still pay money for a handful of
spells," Kathy muttered.

"They'd pay money for colored water and talcum powder,
too." Pandora shrugged. "That doesn't make it right."

"Maybe you can offer matchmaking or something," Kathy
said, studying the beautifully detailed book. "People would
flock to the store for that kind of thing."

For one brief second, the idea of people believing in her enough to flock anywhere filled Pandora with a warm glow. She wanted so badly to offer what the other women in her family had. Comfort, advice, guidance. And a little magic.

Then her shoulders drooped. Because she had no magic to share. Even the one little thing her mother had tried to claim for her had been a failure.

"I'd let people down," she said with a shake of her head. "Hell, when it comes to love stuff, I even let myself down."

"You can't let that asshole ruin your confidence," Kathy growled, lowering the book long enough to glare. "It wasn't your fault your boyfriend was a using, lying criminal."

"Well, it was my fault I let him dupe me, wasn't it? If I was so good at reading people, I'd have seen what was going on. I wouldn't have let the glow of great sex cloud my vision."

Just thinking about it made her stomach hurt.

She'd thought she was in love. She'd fallen for Sean Rafferty hard and fast. The bakery owner's son was everything she'd wanted. Gorgeous. Funny. Sensitive. Her dream guy. She'd thought the fall was mutual, too. Great sex with an up-and-coming pharmacist who seemed crazy about her. He didn't care that she didn't have any special gift. And she hadn't cared that she couldn't seem to get a solid read on his body language. He'd said plenty. Words of love, of admiration.

Then Sean had been busted in an internet prescription scam. And, as if her shock of misreading him that much hadn't been enough, they'd informed her that she was under arrest for collusion. Apparently, her own true love had run his scam using her computer IP address, and then told the police it was all her idea. It'd taken a month, a pile of lawyers' fees and the word of one of Sean's colleagues shooting for a plea deal to convince the cops that she'd been innocent. Clueless, gullible and stupid, but innocent.

His mother firing her had been the final straw. Whether she fit in or not didn't matter, Pandora had needed to come home.

"What's that book?" Kathy asked, clearly trying to distract her from a confidence-busting trip down memory lane.

Pandora gave an absent glance at the book in her lap. Faded ink covered pages that were brittle with age. Some of the writing she recognized as Grammy's. Some she'd never seen before. Then, a tiny flame of excitement kindling in the back of her mind, she flipped the pages. "It's a recipe book."

"Oh."

"Make that *Oh!*" Pandora angled the book to show her friend the handwritten notes above the ingredient list. "These are recipes for aphrodisiacs. Better than love spells, these don't rely on a gift. They just require a talent for cooking."

"Oh, I like that. Maybe you can whip up a tasty aphrodisiac or two for me?" Kathy said with a wicked smile. "I'd be willing to pay a pretty penny for guaranteed good sex."

"Hot and fresh orgasms, delivered to your door in thirty minutes or less?" Pandora joked.

"Sure, why not? Maybe your éclairs aren't quite as amazing as Mrs. Rae's, but you're still a damn good cook. So why not use that? Use those recipes? Put the word out, see what happens. If nothing else, it'll stir up a little curiosity, right?"

It was a crazy idea. Aphrodisiacs? What the hell did Pandora know about sex, let alone sexual aids? The last time she'd seen Sean, he'd been behind bars and, probably for the first time in their relationship, honest when he'd told her that she'd been easy to use because she was naive about sex.

So unless it was a how-to-survive-and-thrive-alone, a do-it-yourself guide to pleasure on a budget, Pandora had very little to offer.

But could she afford to turn away from such a perfect idea?

Her mother would say she'd found this box, this idea, for a reason. Could she take the chance and ignore fate?

Pandora puffed out a breath and looked around the store. This was her heritage. Maybe she didn't have a gift like the rest of the women in her family, but couldn't this be her gift? To save the store?

While her brain was frantically spinning around for an answer, she paced the length of the counter and back. On her third round, Paulie lifted his black head off the carpet to give her the look of patience that only cats have.

"I guess we should do some research," she finally said.

"Don't you have all the recipes you need in that book?"

"I'm sure I do. But I need to find out what kind of food is going to lure in the most customers. Then I can use the recipes to add a special dash of aphrodisiac delight."

As she reached under the counter to get a notepad and pen so she and Kathy could brainstorm, she had to shake her head.

Wasn't it ironic? It was because of sex that she'd had to run home and now sex was going to be the thing that saved that home.

Two months later

"I NEED A FAVOR... A sexual favor, you might say."

The words were so low, they almost faded into the dull cacophony of the bar's noise. Pool cues smacking balls and the occasional fist smacking a face were typical in this low-end dive. Sexual favors were plentiful, too, but usually they involved the back room and cash in advance.

Caleb Black arched a brow and took a slow sip of his beer before saying, "That's not the way I roll, but Christmas is coming. Want me to slap a bow on the ass of one of those fancy blow-up dolls and call it your present?"

Hunter's dead-eyed look didn't intimidate, but it did make Caleb hide his smirk in his beer. Caleb was known far and wide as a hard-ass dude with a bad attitude. But when he was around Hunter, he came off as sweetness and light on a sugar high.

The man was a highly trained FBI special agent swiftly rising in the ranks thanks to his brilliant mind, killer instincts and vicious right hook.

He was also Caleb's college roommate and oldest, most trusted friend. Which meant poking at that steely resolve was mandatory.

"Okay, crossing blow-up doll off my shopping list," Caleb decided. "But you should know that my sexual favors don't come cheap."

"From what I've heard, dirt cheap is more like it."

Caleb's smirk didn't change. When a man was as good as he was with women, he didn't need to defend his record. Knowing Hunter would get to the point in his own good time, Caleb leaned back, the chair creaking as he crossed his ankle over his knee and waited.

Always quick on the uptake, Hunter pushed his barely touched beer aside and leaned forward, his hands loose on the scarred table between them. Even in the dim bar light, his eyes shone with an intensity that told Caleb the guy was gonna try to sucker him in.

But Caleb had learned suckering at his daddy's knee.

"You're coming off a big case, right?" Hunter confirmed.

Not quite the tact he'd expected. But it wasn't his game, so Caleb just nodded. And waited.

"Word is you've hit burnout. That you're taking some time off to consider your options."

The smirk didn't shift on Caleb's face. But his entire body tensed. He wasn't a sharing kind of guy. He hadn't told anyone he was burning out except his direct superior, who'd sworn to keep it to himself.

"Word sounds like a gossipy, giggling teenager," was all Caleb said, though. "Who's the gossip and when did you start listening to that kind of crap?"

"It's amazing how much information you can pick up through speculation." Hunter sidestepped. "So while you're considering those options, maybe you might be interested in doing a friend a favor?"

"I'm more interested in lying on a beach in Cabo with half-naked women licking coconut-flavored oil off my body," Caleb mused, taking another swig of beer.

"What if I used the owe-me card?" Hunter asked quietly, his gaze steady on Caleb's. Intimidation 101.

Last week, Caleb had faced down a Colombian drug lord who'd preferred to blow up the building he stood in than be arrested when he found out his newest right-hand man was actually DEA.

It would take a lot more than 101 to make Caleb squirm.

Then again, he did owe Hunter. Back in their first year of college, Caleb had been a better con than a student. Overwhelmed by the realities of college life, he'd cheated on his midterm psych project. Hunter had caught him. He didn't threaten to turn him in. He didn't lecture. He simply threw Caleb's own dreams back in his face until he'd cracked, then helped him pull together a new project. He hadn't snagged the A he'd hoped for, but Caleb had found a new sense of pride he'd never known.

Shit.

Caleb hated unpaid debts. Especially sappy emotional ones.

"Cut the bullshit and get to the point," he suggested.

Realizing he'd won, Hunter didn't gloat. He just leaned back in his chair and took a sip of his own beer. "You're from a small town in the Santa Cruz Mountains, right? Black Oak, California."

It wasn't a question, but Caleb inclined his head.

"You still have family there."

"Maybe." Probably. He knew his sister was living just outside of San Francisco, playing the good girl. And who the hell knew where his brother was. A chip off the ole block, Gabriel was probably fleecing some rich widow of her wedding ring. But their father's family had founded Black Oak, and while Tobias Black hadn't ever gone for the political game, he'd always kept his fingers on the strings of his hometown.

But Caleb hadn't lived there since he'd left for college twelve years before. And he hadn't been back at all since he'd graduated and joined the DEA.

Eight years before, two months before Caleb had graduated, they'd had one helluva family brawl. Ugly accusations, bitter recriminations and vicious ultimatums.

Tobias Black had raised his three kids alone when his wife had died, keeping the family tighter than peas in one very conniving pod. But with that explosion, they'd all gone their separate ways. Caleb had grown up with an almost smothering sense of family. These days he was more like an orphan.

Just as well. Spending time with Tobias was an emotional pain in the ass at best, a conflict of interest at worst.

"It's an interesting little town. Quaint even. Your maternal aunt is the mayor, but word is that it's actually your father who runs the town. Tobias Black, a known con artist with a huge FBI file and no convictions. Estimates of his take over the years is in the millions. And even knowing he was behind some of the major scams of the century, they've never gathered enough evidence to convict him."

Arching his brow, Hunter paused. Caleb just shrugged. So his dad was damn good at what he did. Maybe it was wrong to feel pride in the old man, given Caleb's dedication to the law. But you had to admire the guy for his skills.

"Five years ago, for no apparent reason, Tobias Black pulled out of the con games. He reputedly went straight, focusing his attention on his motorcycle shop and the small town he calls his own."

"You're saying a whole bunch of stuff we both know. Why don't you get to the part where you fill me in on the stuff I don't."

"For the last few months, we've been getting reports of a new drug. Some new form of MOMA."

"Ecstasy?" Caleb pushed his beer away since they appeared to be getting down to business. "What's new about it?"

"It's been refined. Higher-grade ingredients, some obscure herbs that counteract a few of the side effects."

"Herbs? Like, what? Holistic shit?"

"Right. Not a major change, really. Enough to give sellers the 'healthier choice' pitch, but that's about it. The problem stems from the addition of pheromones."

Eight years in the DEA had told Caleb that just when he'd thought he'd seen and heard everything, some clever asshole would come up with a new twist to screw with the human body. He sighed and shook his head. "So not only does it give the user a cheap sexual zing, but they can drag unsuspecting suckers down with them?"

"Pretty much. As far as the labs can tell, it's not a high enough grade to classify as a date-rape drug, but the potential is there."

The potential to make things worse was always there. Once upon a time, Caleb had figured he could make a difference. But he'd been wrong. After years of fighting drugs in the ugly underbelly of society, Caleb was pretty much done waging the useless battle. He'd turned in his resignation two days ago, but his boss had refused to accept it. Instead, he'd told Caleb to take some time off. To go home, visit family, come out of deep cover for a few months and reconnect with himself before he made any major decisions.

The only piece of that advice Caleb had planned to take was the time off.

He noted the rigid set of Hunter's jaw, then met the man's steady gaze and gave an inward sigh. Looked as if he was wrong on that count, too.

"Can't you feebs get in there on your own?" he asked. The bureau didn't have the same mandate as the DEA, but still, they should have the resources to go in themselves.

"Let's just say I'd rather use my own resources first."

Caleb nodded. He'd figured it was something like that. Second-generation FBI, Hunter had a rep for playing outside the tangled strings of bureaucracy more often than not. His close rate was so high, though, that the higher-ups tended to ignore his unorthodox habits.

"You're looking at Black Oak as the supply center. Have you narrowed down any suspects?"

Caleb wasn't a fool. He knew where Hunter was going with this. But he wasn't biting. He'd pony up whatever info he had on the town that might help the case, but that was it. He wasn't going back to Black Oak.

Which Hunter damn well knew. One drunken college night, Caleb had opened up enough to share how much he hated his father, how glad he'd been to get the hell out of Black Oak. And how he'd vowed, once he'd left, to never return.

"Black Oak appears to be the supply center, yes. But that's not the big issue for me." For the first time since he'd strode into the bar and sat across from Caleb, Hunter's eyes slid away. Just for a second. That's all it took, though, to let Caleb know he wasn't going to like whatever came next.

No matter. Wasn't much about life these days he did like.

Still, he took a swig of the beer. Never hurt to be prepared.

"We've tracked the source. As far as we can tell, there's only one suspect."

Caleb waited silently. Most people, when faced with six feet two inches of brooding intimidation blurted out secrets faster than a gumball machine spewed candy. But Hunter wasn't most people.

"A reliable source tipped me to the suspect."

Caleb dropped the chair back on all four legs, bracing himself.

"Tobias Black."

Caleb mentally reared back as if he'd taken a fist to the face. He managed to keep his actual reaction contained to a wince, though. So much for bracing himself.

"He's out of the game," Caleb said, throwing Hunter's own words back at him. He didn't know if it was true, though. Sure, his father might claim he'd quit the con, gone straight. But the only thing Tobias was better at than playing the game was lying. Still, while cons were one thing, drugs were an ugly place Tobias wouldn't go.

"He's been making noises lately." Hunter's dark gaze was steady as he watched Caleb.

"Noises don't equal manufacturing drugs."

Hunter just stared.

Fuck.

"It's not his style," Caleb said, none of his frustration coming through in his tone. "I'm not defending him—without a doubt, he's a crook, a con and a shill. The man's spent his life pulling swindle after scam. But he operates on his own. Drugs come with partners. Unreliable, unpredictable partners."

Which had been the crux of his family's explosion. Tobias had found himself a lady friend. A lonely widower, he'd become a cliché, falling hard for a nice rack and promises made between the sheets. She must have been damn good, because she'd blinded the king of cons into letting her into his game. Fifty-fifty split.

His little sister, Maya, had screamed betrayal, claiming her father cared more about his bimbo than his own kids, the memory of his late wife and the legacy they'd built together.

His younger brother, Gabriel, had been pissed over losing half the take.

Caleb had just seen it as a sign to get the hell out.

He ignored Hunter's arched brow. For the first time since sitting down, Caleb looked away. His gaze rested on the mirrored wall behind Hunter. In it, he could see the tattoo on his own biceps. The sharp, snarling teeth of the lone wolf was clearly visible beneath the black sleeve of his T-shirt.

A teenager's ode to the father he'd worshipped before the idol had fallen. An adult's acceptance of the simple fact of life—that he could depend on no one.

"What do you want me to do?" Caleb asked, swinging his eyes back to Hunter.

"Just nose around. You can get into town, get close to the right people, without arousing suspicion. Nobody there, other than your father, knows you're DEA, right?"

Caleb shrugged. "Most think I'm the lowlife I use as a cover. The rest probably figure I was shivved in prison years ago."

"That'll work."

Caleb sighed. He could walk away. It wasn't his gig and nobody was pulling his strings. But Hunter's accusation was a game changer. Whatever went down, Caleb would be the one uncovering the truth. How or what he'd do with it, he had no clue.

"I'm not making any promises," Caleb said. "Dear ole dad

isn't much for welcoming the prodigal back into the fold, you know."

"I have faith in your powers of persuasion."

Caleb smirked, tilting his beer bottle in thanks. "You're buying."

"One last question," Hunter said as Caleb pushed back from the table.

"Yeah?"

"Do you really do Christmas shopping?" For the first time that night, emotion showed on Hunter's face. Skepticism with a dash of amusement.

"Yeah. But now you can consider this little favor your gift, instead of the blow-up doll." Caleb stood, shrugging into his worn denim jacket. "She was a nice one, too. Vibrated and everything."

2

A LUNCH-LADEN TRAY held high over her head, Pandora nodded at Fifi's frantic signal to let her know she'd make her way into the store as soon as she could.

Rehiring Fifi, a young blonde as cute as her name, was the second smartest thing Pandora had done since she'd taken over the store. The first, of course, was to serve up the promise of hot sex.

She wound her way through the throng of customers packing the solarium attached to the back of the store. It was amazing how a few tables, some chairs and minimal investment had transformed what two months ago had been storage into Pandora's brainchild, the Moonspun Café.

All it'd taken was a list of her skills, a couple bottles of wine with Kathy and a huge hunk of Pandora's favorite seven-layer chocolate cake to nail down the details. She'd spent years off and on working in restaurants. She was a really good pastry chef, but sandwiches and salads had been an easy enough thing to add to the menu.

Between Great-Grammy's cookbooks, a list of foods reputed to be aphrodisiacs and the judicious start of a few rumors, and she'd launched the lunch-only venture last month.

And it was a hit. If this kept up, Pandora was thinking about starting a little mail-order business. Sexy sweets, aphrodisiac-laced treats for lovers. A great idea, if she did say so herself. And—*ha!*—one that didn't require any special family talent.

She grinned and shifted the heavy tray off her shoulder.

"Here you go, the Hot-Cha-Cha Chicken on toasted sourdough for two, a side of French-kissing fries and ginseng-over-ice tea," she recited as she set the aphrodisiac-laced lunch order on the small iron table between a couple of octogenarians giving each other googly eyes.

Pandora carefully kept her gaze above the table as she smiled into the couple's wrinkled faces. Yesterday, she'd bent down to pick up a dropped fork and saw more than she'd bargained for. She'd never be able to look librarian Loretta and the office-supply delivery guy in the eye again after seeing Loretta fondle his dewy decimals.

"This looks lovely, dear," said the elderly woman, who's granddaughter had babysat Pandora back in the day. The woman giggled and shot the age-freckled man across from her a naughty look before adding, "You'll bring us up a slice of the molten hot-chocolate cake, won't you?"

"Wrap that cake up to go," the gentleman said, his voice huge in his frail body. "We've got a little siesta loving planned."

Pandora tried not to wince. She loved how well this little venture was taking off, but holy cow! She sure wished people wouldn't equate her making their sexy treats with wanting to hear the resulting deets.

Proving that wishes rarely came true, Mrs. Sellers leaned closer and whispered, "Since you started serving up these yummy lunches, I haven't had to fake it once. This stuff is better than Viagra. Now my sweet Merv, here, is a sex maniac."

Ack, there were so many kinds of wrong in that sentence, Pandora couldn't even wrap her mind around it. Trying to block the images the words inspired, she winced and shook her head so fast her hair got stuck in her eyelashes. "No. Oh, no, Mrs. Sellers. Don't thank me."

"Don't be modest, young lady. You've done so much for the sex drive of Black Oak as a whole. Not just us seniors, either. I heard Lola, my daughter's hairdresser who can't be much older than you, telling the gals at the salon how you've saved her marriage with your mead- and sexy-spiced chocolate-dipped strawberries."

What was she supposed to say to that? All she could come up with was a weak smile and a murmured thanks. She caught Fifi's wave again and held up one finger to let the girl know she was on her way.

"My favorites are those sweet-nothings ginger cookies, Pandora. I'd ask for your recipe, but I know you put a little something special in there. You have your gramma's magic touch, don't you?" Mrs. Sellers joked, poking a bony elbow into Pandora's thigh. "Your mom must have been so happy to have you come back to Black Oak. Are you running the store on your own now?"

"Mom's thrilled," Pandora said, the memory of Cassiopeia's excitement at her daughter's plans to save the store filling her with joy. "But if you'll excuse me, I need to check in with Fifi. Don't forget to look over the fabulous specials for the holiday season. We're offering a Christmas discount in the store for our diners, if you wanted to do a little shopping."

With another smile for her favorite elderly couple, Pandora gratefully excused herself and hurried over to the wide, bead-draped doorway that separated Moonspun Dreams' retail side from the café.

"What's wrong?" Pandora asked.

Two months ago, whenever she'd asked that question it was because the store seemed to be spiraling into failure. She'd been freaked about vendors demanding payment, customers complaining about a lack of variety in the tarot card stock or, on one horrific occasion, a mouse so big it had scared the cats.

In the past five weeks, Moonspun Dreams had done a one-eighty. Now she had vendors begging her to take two-for-one discounts, customers complaining about waiting in too long a line and the health department stopping in for lunch.

And yet, her trepidation of that question hadn't lessened one iota. Funny how that worked.

"Nothing's wrong," Fifi said, her smile huge as she bounced on the balls of her feet like a kid about to sit on Santa's lap. "Sheriff Hottie's here again. Lucky girl, this is the third time he's been in this week. He's the best catch in Black Oak. And he's here to see you."

Pandora's smile was just a little stiff. It wasn't that she had anything against Sheriff Hottie, otherwise known as Jeff Kendall. He was a nice guy. A former class president, Jeff had an affable sort of charm that half the women in town were crazy about. She glanced over to where he was chatting with a shaggy-haired guy who kept coming in to moon over Fifi and winced.

She had no idea why he rubbed her wrong. Her mother would claim it was intuition or her gift for reading people. But Pandora knew she had neither.

Christmas carols crooned softly through the speakers, singing messages of hope as she crossed the room. It took a minute, since the space was filled with shoppers, quite a few with questions.

"Sheriff," she greeted as she stepped behind the counter. She offered him a friendly smile, then folded her hands together before he could offer to shake one. "What can I do for you today?"

He gave her an appreciative glance and a friendly smile that made it easy to see why the town called him Sheriff Hottie. Blue eyes sparkled and a manly dimple winked. Still, a part of her wished she could be back in the café, listening to Mrs. Sellers share the details of her last passionate excursion with Merv the sex maniac.

"Pandora, looks like business is booming nicely for a weekday," he observed, his eyes on her rather than the store. He was tall, easily six feet, and still carried the same nice build that'd made him a star quarterback in school. "Cassiopeia must be thrilled. Is she coming home soon?"

Having combined her yearly spiritual sabbatical with the psychics' conference, Cassiopeia was still in Sedona, Arizona. Pandora's mother was, hopefully, too busy balancing her chi to be worrying about the store.

"She's due home by Yule," Pandora answered. At his puzzled glance, she amended it to, "The week before Christmas."

"Ah, gotcha. Your mom is really into that New Agey stuff, isn't she?"

Pandora just shrugged. She wanted to hide away from that friendly look. There was no innuendo, no rudeness, but she still felt dirty. Instead, she made a show of lifting Bonnie, cuddling her close so that the cat was a furry curtain between Pandora's body and the sheriff's gaze.

"My mother's interests are many-faceted. Right now, I'm sure if she were here, she'd be asking if you'd finished your holiday shopping, Sheriff. We're running a few specials in the café and have a stocking-stuffer sale on tumbled stones and crystals today. Maybe you'd like to check it out?"

"Maybe. But I'm thinking if I did all my shopping now, I wouldn't have an excuse to come back and visit you every day," he said, putting a heavy dose of flirt in his tone. Leaning one elbow on the counter, he gave her a smoldering look before he glanced at the shoppers milling around, many with wicker baskets filled with merchandise swinging on their arms.

"I really am blown away by how you've increased business here," he said. "That whole aphrodisiac angle is really drawing them in, isn't it? How'd you come up with that? Don't tell me it's from personal experience or I might have a heart attack."

His flirty grin was easy, the look in his eyes friendly and fun. Pandora still inwardly cringed.

"Actually," she corrected meticulously, her fingers defiantly combing through the soft, fluffy fur of the cat, "the recipes have been handed down from my great-grandmother. Do you remember her? She's the one with all the experience."

Pandora tried not to smirk when his smile dimmed a little. Nothing like offering up the image of a white-haired old lady to diffuse a guy's sexy talk.

"How about dinner Friday night?" he said. "I'll pick you up at seven and you can tell me all about your great-grandma and her recipes."

What a stubborn man. But she was just as stubborn. She knew she had no reason to refuse—that she was getting a weird vibe wasn't good enough—but still, Pandora shook her head.

"I'm sorry, but no," she told him. Then, seeing the disappointment in his gaze, she tried to soften her words with a smile.

"I really wish you'd change your mind," Sheriff Kendall said, reaching over Bonnie to give Pandora's cheek a teasing sort of pinch. She gasped, her fingers clenching the cat's fur. Whether it was in protest, or because the sheriff was just too close, Bonnie hissed and leaped from Pandora's arms.

"I'm sorry," she said again, stepping back so she and her

cheek were out of reach. "I'm trying to focus on the store right now. I need to get us back on our feet before I start thinking about dating."

"Okay. I understand." He offered that friendly smile again and turned to go. Then he looked back. "Just so you know, though, I plan to keep coming back until I change your mind."

Crap.

She waited until he stepped over Paulie, who carpeted the welcome mat like a boneless blanket of fur, and watched him slide behind the wheel of the police cruiser he'd parked to blocking the door. Then she almost wilted as the tension she hadn't realized was tying her in knots seeped from her shoulders.

"No offense, boss, but you're crazy," Fifi declared, stepping next to Pandora and offering a sad shake of her head. "I'd do anything to date the sexy sheriff. I can't believe you turned him down."

What was she supposed to say? That her internal warning system was screaming out against the guy? That same system had hummed like a happy kitten over Sean.

So obviously, the system sucked.

She gave Fifi a tiny grimace and said, "I guess I might have been a little hasty turning him down."

"A little? More like a lot crazy. Dude's a serious heart-throb."

Pandora grinned as the blonde gave her heart a thump-thumping pat.

"Okay," she decided, squaring her shoulders against the sick feeling in her stomach. Just nerves about dipping back into the dating pond, she was sure. "I'll tell you what. The next time he asks, I'll say yes."

Fifi's cheer garnered a few stares and a lot of smiles, especially from the young man with shaggy brown hair who was watching her like an adoring puppy.

Well, there you have it, Pandora decided with a grin of her own. The town obviously approved.

Ten minutes later, Pandora was ringing up a customer and still worrying over whether Sean had ruined her for all men, when a sugary-sweet voice grated down her spine.

"My mother said there was a blown-glass piece in here she thought I'd like as a Christmas gift. She probably mixed up the store names again, though, poor dear. I don't see anything in here I need."

Crap. Pandora took a deep breath, gesturing with her chin for Fifi to close up the café for her. This would probably take a while. She'd gone to high school with Lilah Gomez, and eight years later the other woman still held the privilege of being Pandora's least favorite person—which, given the events of this last year, was really saying something.

Knowing the importance of not showing weakness to her sworn enemy, she cleared her face of all expression and turned to the brunette.

"Your mother has excellent taste. Too bad she didn't pass it, and the ability to dress appropriately, on to her only daughter," Pandora said sweetly. She made a show of looking the other woman up and down, taking in her red pleather tunic with its low-cut, white fur-trimmed neckline that showed off her impressively expensive breasts. She raised a brow at the shimmery black leggings and a pair of do-me heeled boots that would make any dominatrix proud. "What do you call this look? Holiday hussy?"

"I'm the customer here. Why don't you put on your cute-little-clerk hat and show me whatever overpriced joke my mother saw so I can reject it and go shop in a real store."

"From where I'm standing, which is right next to the cash register, in the handful of times you've been in Moonspun

Dreams you've never bought a single thing. So you're not a customer. You're a loiterer."

Lilah responded with a haughty look. She'd never bothered with her frenemy act before. Probably because she knew that Pandora would see right through it. Instead, the brunette leaned both elbows on the counter and bent forward to say under her breath, "You'd know crime, now, wouldn't you? What was it you were busted for? Something to do with drugs? Or was it lying?"

The only thing that persuaded Pandora to unclench her teeth was the fact that she couldn't afford to get them fixed if one broke. Instead, she turned on the heel of her own unslutty boots and retrieved a blown-glass peacock, each feather shimmering delicately in the light.

Before she'd even set the piece on the counter, she could see the covetous spark in Lilah's eyes. But instead of saying she liked it, the other woman turned her nose to the air and gave a sniff.

"It's okay. Just the kind of thing I'd expect to find in this dingy little store."

"The artist is one of my mother's clients," Pandora said, surreptitiously scraping the sale sticker off the price tag. She'd be damned if Lilah was getting thirty percent off. "Her work is currently in the White House and was recently featured in a George Clooney movie."

Drool formed in the corner of Lilah's heavily painted mouth. Her hand was halfway to her purse before she thought to ask, "How much is it?"

The desire to make a sale warred with the desire to kick the bitchy woman out of the store. But responsibility always trumped personal satisfaction for Pandora. Which was probably why women like Lilah, and Cassiopeia, Fifi and even old Mrs. Sellers, had a lot more fun that she did.

With one unvarnished fingernail, she pushed the price tag across the counter. Lilah's eyes rounded and her lips drooped.

"Will you hold it? My mother hinted that she'd get it for me as a Christmas gift."

"You want me to hold an overpriced joke?"

The woman's glare was vicious, but she jerked her chin in affirmation.

Hey, that was fun. Maybe all Cassiopeia's lectures about karma were true.

Before Pandora could decide whether to go for gracious or gloating, a loud roaring rumbled through the air.

She and Lilah both stared as a huge Harley slowed down, the helmeted rider turning his head to stare into the store. A shiver skittered between Pandora's shoulder blades. Another out-of-towner? Usually tourism went dry in Black Oak between Thanksgiving and Valentine's. It was probably someone visiting Custom Rides, the motorcycle shop that backed up to Moonspun.

"Company?" Fifi speculated, coming in from the café to stare, too.

"Must have heard about the yippee-skippy you're offering up," Mrs. Sellers predicted, heading out the door hand in hand with her tottering hunk of afternoon delight.

As one, Pandora sighed and Lilah sneered.

"That's disgusting," Lilah muttered.

"What is? The idea of two people enjoying each other's company?"

"You know they're sneaking off to have sex," the woman said, hissing the last word as if it were pure evil. The overblown brunette averted her eyes from the elderly couple as though she was worried that they wouldn't hold out until they toddled all the way to their love nest, instead giving in and doing the nasty right there in the doorway.

"And sex is bad... Why?" Pandora put on her most obnoxious, innocently sweet smile. "From what I heard, you were having it a couple nights ago. Wasn't it in the backseat of an old Nova parked behind Lander's Market?"

Fifi giggled, forcing Lilah to split her glare between the two women.

Before she could spill her ire, though, the chimes over the door sang. And in walked Pandora's worst nightmare. The sexiest man she'd ever seen, wearing black leather and a dangerous attitude. The kind of guy who could make her forget her own name, right along with her convictions, her vow of chastity and where she'd left her underpants.

Black hair swept back from a face worthy of a *GQ* cover. Sharp cheekbones, a chiseled, hair-roughened chin and vivid gold eyes topped broad shoulders and long, denim-clad legs that seemed to go on forever.

Pandora's hormones sighed in appreciation as desire flared, smoking hot, in her belly. She wanted to leap over the counter and slide that leather jacket off those wide shoulders and see up close and personal if his chest and arms lived up to the promise of the rest of his body.

"Oh, my," Fifi breathed.

"Hubba hubba," Lilah moaned.

"Go away," Pandora muttered.

The guy paused just inside the door, then knelt down to give Paulie's head a quick rub before straightening and looking around. His narrowed gaze seemed to take in everything in one quick glance. Then his eyes locked on Pandora's. Nerves battled with lust as she felt something deep inside click. A recognition. And that soul-deep terror that this was a man who spelled trouble in every way possible.

"Ladies," Caleb greeted, barely aware of the two women on his side of the counter. His eyes were glued on the sweet little dish on the other side.

Her hair, a dark auburn so deep it looked like mahogany, tumbled over her shoulders in a silken slide, the tips waving over the sweet curve of her breasts. She wore a simple white shirt that draped gently over her curves instead of hugging them, and tiny silver earrings that made her look like a sweet-faced innocent. From the fresh-faced look, she didn't have any makeup on, either. Or maybe it just seemed that way because she was standing next to a gal who troweled it on like spackle.

"Well, hello there," Spackle Gal said. The brunette, dressed as if she moonlighted on the stroll, minced her way across the floor to lay a red-taloned hand on his arm. "It's a pleasure to have you here in Black Oak. I'm the welcome wagon, and I'd be happy to show you a good time while you're visiting our little town."

His brow arched, Caleb glanced at her hand, then back at her face. It only took her a second to get a clue and move her fingers back where they belonged.

"I know the town just fine, thanks," he dismissed. His gaze went back to the sweetie behind the counter. "Apparently I don't know everyone in town as well as I'd like, though."

The brunette gave a little hiss. Caleb ignored her. Despite her clear message of a free-and-easy good time, he wasn't interested.

He'd only come in to check the place out. Not because he was interested in… He looked around, wondering what the hell they sold here. This store shared the alley with what was apparently his father's motorcycle shop. His dad had still been on the take when Caleb had lived in Black Oak, so his shop was new, and Caleb's familiarity with this side of town sketchy.

So this weird store was going to be his new home away from home. By hanging here he could scope things out. Get the lay of the land, keep low for a few days and see how much intel he could scout. Then he'd decide if he wanted to let Tobias know he was in town or not.

"Some people aren't as important to know as others," the brunette said, trying her luck again by nudging close enough to press one impressive breast against his arm. Caleb was grateful for the extra protection of his leather jacket. "Why don't you and I go to Mick's for a drink and I'll introduce you around."

Caleb wanted to sigh. God, he was tired. Undercover standard operating procedure said take her offer. She was the perfect cover. A resident who probably liked her gossip, she could fill him in on all the townspeople. As blatantly sexual as she was, she might even have an in with the ecstasy crowd.

She'd obviously be happy to offer up any manner of information, favors and probably kinky acts, and walk away with a smile and no regrets the next morning. But he was tired of using himself, losing himself, like that.

And, dammit, he was supposed to be on vacation. A man shouldn't feel guilty about turning down cheap sex while he was on vacation.

"I'm good," he said, stepping away to make his rejection clear. From her glare, she got the message loud and clear. Color high on her cheeks, she shot an ugly look at the girls standing at the counter before heading for the door.

"You might want to slow down on testing your wares from the café, Pandora," the vamp warned over her shoulder as she teetered out of the store. "Not only is that aphrodisiac crap in danger of making you sound like a slut, but you're gaining weight."

Caleb's eyes cut to the women behind the counter, noting the shocked horror in the blonde's eyes and the sneer on the redhead's face. He grinned, liking her screw-you attitude.

"What's she so bitchy about?" he asked, keeping his smile friendly. Nothing connected with a mark—or suspect—faster than sympathy. Besides, facts were facts…the woman had been a bitch. He wandered the store ostensibly looking at merchandise while eyeing the back wall and its bead-covered doorway.

"That's her default personality," the redhead said.

"Pandora, is it?"

He wondered why she was looking at him as if he was a wolf about to pounce. Sure, he'd been a troublemaker as a teen, but he'd been gone almost twelve years. Was his rep still that bad in Black Oak? He didn't recognize her. Younger than him, she was closer to his sister's age.

"Hello?" he said, giving her a verbal nudge as he picked up a clear rock shaped like a pyramid, pretending to inspect it. Her worried stare was starting to bug him.

"I'll go make sure everyone's out of the café since it's closed now," the blonde murmured.

"Yes, I'm Pandora," the other woman said, grabbing the arm of the blonde before she could move away. "I'm the, um, owner. Can I help you?"

"Owner? You don't sound so sure."

"I'm still getting used to the idea." Pandora's smile was as stiff and fake as the blow-up doll Caleb had shipped off to Hunter the previous day. "What can I do for you?"

God, so many things. Let him taste those lips to see if they were as soft and delicious as they looked. Slide that silky-looking hair over his naked body. Tell him about all her favorite sexual positions and give him a chance to teach her his.

"I'm just looking around. You've got a nice place here."

"Thanks. Was there anything specific you were shopping for?"

His grin said it all. A sweet pink flush colored her cheeks, but he saw the flash of reciprocated interest in her eyes. Then, for some bizarre reason, she slammed that door shut with an impersonal arch of her brow.

What the hell? Unlike his brother, Gabriel, he didn't expect women to fall at his feet. And the hard-to-get game did have appeal sometimes. But to totally deny the attraction? What was up with that?

Focus, Black, he reminded himself. He'd come to town for a crappy reason and wanted to leave as fast as he could. So her denial was a good thing.

And maybe if he told himself that a few hundred more times, he'd believe it.

"So you have a café here, too?" he asked, poking through a basket of glossy rocks and trying to take his own advice to focus. Now that he was closer, he noted the noise and tasty scents coming through that beaded curtain. Was the back door to the alley through there?

Before he could poke his head through to see, a group of people strode out with a clatter of beads and a lot of laughter. They'd obviously been having a happy holiday lunch.

There, in the center of the group like a king surrounded by his royal court, was Tobias Black. His lion's mane of black hair had gone gray at the temples. His face sported a few more wrinkles, adding to its austere authority. Still tall and lean, he wore jeans and biker boots, a denim work shirt and a mellow smile.

Caleb froze. Control broke for a brief second as he closed his eyes against the crashing waves of memories as they pounded through his head—and his heart. Holidays and hugs, lectures and encouraging winks. Watching his dad pull a con, then pulling his first con while his dad watched. The trip to Baskin-Robbins afterward, where Tobias let Caleb treat to hot-fudge sundaes with his ill-gotten gains, cementing the lesson that winning was sweet, but the money had to be kept in circulation.

And then his last day of college. The day when Caleb had told dear ole dad that he was bucking family tradition and basically becoming the enemy. A cop. And when he'd threatened, in cocky righteousness, that if his dad didn't dump his new partner and go straight, Caleb was leaving the family. That'd been the point his dad had told him to get his ass out.

Good times.

Caleb took a deep breath, his eyes meeting the wide hazel gaze of the pretty redhead behind the counter. He frowned at the sympathy and concern on her face. In the past eight years, he'd faced down whacked-out drug addicts and homicidal drug lords for a living with a blank face. Why did this pretty little thing think there was anything to be sympathetic over? Something to mull over later. Right now he had to pay the piper.

Caleb slowly turned around, automatically shoving his hands into the front pockets of his jeans and rocking back on his heels. He'd known this moment would come, but now that it had, he wasn't ready. He'd walked away from his family and used that lack of emotional ties in building his career. But now he was back, face-to-face with his father.

And he had no idea how he felt about it.

Like a bull who'd suddenly hit a steel wall, Tobias slammed to a halt. His midnight-blue eyes went huge. But only for a second. Then he grinned. A charming grin that Caleb knew was hiding that shock he hadn't meant to show.

"Well, well," Tobias said, slowly walking forward. "What have we here? If it isn't the prodigal son."

3

OH, MY. MR. TALL, HOT and Dangerous was one of the wild and mysterious Black clan? Along with the rest of the gawpers standing around the store, Pandora stared, rapt, as the two men faced off.

"Wow," Fifi breathed.

Pandora nodded. Wow, indeed.

The Black clan was legend. History said a Black had founded the small town a hundred years back. But for all their standing in the town, people still passed rumors and innuendo in whispers, wondering where the Black fortune came from. Everything from inheriting from an eccentric relative to robbing banks to wise investments. All anyone knew for sure was that they were the wealthiest family in Black Oak, that Tobias's wife had died of leukemia before his youngest child could walk, and until five years ago when Tobias had opened a custom motorcycle shop, they hadn't appeared to work for a living.

"I'm surprised to see you here," Tobias was saying. Pandora frowned, though. The older man didn't look so much surprised as... What? She studied his body language, the way he rocked back on his heels, the set of his shoulders. If she had to guess, she'd say he looked satisfied.

"I didn't realize I had to check in with you as soon as I crossed the city limits," Caleb returned.

"Check in?" Tobias's hearty laugh filled the store, making half the customers smile in response. "Son, you know I don't make rules like that. But if I'd known you were gonna be in town for the holidays, I'd have had Mrs. Long get your room ready."

Caleb's only response was an arched brow.

Pandora tensed. They seemed amiable enough, but she still felt as if she was watching a boxing match. The two men circled each other without even moving. The gorgeously sexy biker looked even more dangerous than he had when he'd walked in. On the surface, he was relaxed, leaning against the wall. She could see the bored look on his narrow face and the general sense of *screw-you* surrounding him. But his feet gave him away. Instead of crossed at the ankle, or rocked back on the heels, his boots were planted as if he were ready to run.

This reunion was a family thing. Private. Especially if one of them decided to throw a punch.

"Maybe the two of you would like some privacy," she offered. The customers turned as one, a few shooting her guilty looks while the rest glared. Black Oak loved its gossip.

"No." Caleb shook his head before stepping forward to lay a warm, strong hand on Pandora's arm. The only thing that kept her from gasping and scurrying away was a desperate need to not add more fuel to the already out-of-control whisperfest brewing.

"We need to talk, son," Tobias insisted. His words were quiet, they were friendly and they were offered with a smile. They were also hard as steel.

"Maybe later," Caleb dismissed them. "Right now Pandora's promised me lunch."

"What?" she yelped. Caleb's fingers tightened on her arm.

"Really?" Tobias said at the same time, drawing the word out and giving them both a toothy smile.

Rock, meet hard place. Pandora's eyes swept the store, noting the slew of avid townspeople staring, waiting to see what she did. A few even mouthed the words *stay here.* Even the cats were watching her, Bonnie with her head tilted in curiosity, Paulie peering at her through slitted eyes, as if she was disturbing his nap. Then her gaze met Caleb's.

His eyes didn't beg. His face was passive. He simply returned her stare, his eyes steady. She could only hold his look for a few seconds, the intensity of those gold eyes sending crazy swirls of sexual heat spiraling down through her belly.

"Um, yes. Lunch," she murmured, finally pulling her arm out from under his hand. Needing to move, she headed toward the café.

Caleb sauntered beside her, his long legs easily keeping up with her rushed steps.

Everyone in the store moved, too. Apparently, customers were positioning themselves for the best view into the café.

Tobias, however, followed them right through the beads.

"I'm so glad to see so many holiday shoppers," Pandora called back through the beaded doorway of the café. "I know Cassiopeia will be thrilled when I tell her who was in buying merchandise today."

That got them going. Customers scurried to shelves, displays and tables in search of something to keep the town woo-woo queen from cursing them. Or worse, not giving them a peek into their future the next time they asked.

"I'm sure Pandora won't mind if we have a little chat before lunch," Tobias said.

She shook her head no, and was about to offer to wait in the kitchen, when Caleb laid his hand on her arm again.

She froze. Her breath caught and her legs went weak at his touch. The guy wasn't even looking at her and she was about to melt into a puddle at his feet. While his only use for her was to avoid talking to his daddy.

Yep, he was bad news.

Needing to unfog her brain, and unlust her body, she stepped away.

"I'm just passing through," Caleb said, leaning casually against the wall. But the smirk he shot Pandora was amused, as if he knew exactly what kind of effect he had on her.

"How long until you passed through my front door?" Tobias challenged. "You were going to let me know you were in town, weren't you?"

Silence. The hottie had that intense, brooding rebellious thing down pat. Without him saying a word, Pandora knew he hadn't planned to see his father, would have preferred that dear ole dad didn't even know he was in town and was thoroughly pissed to be put in the position of defending himself.

The air in the café was heavy with tension. So out of her element she wanted to turn heel and run all the way back to San Francisco, Pandora shifted from one foot to the other, forcing herself to stay in place.

"Today's special is a hot and spicy double meatball sandwich and four-layer Foreplay Chocolate Cake for dessert," she blurted out in her perkiest waitress voice.

It wasn't until both men shot her identical looks of shocked amusement that she realized what she'd offered. Oh, hell. She wanted to smack her hand over her mouth in horror. Her lust for Caleb was bad enough, but for it to sneak out in front of his father?

"I mean, um, that's the menu. Not an offer, you know? I wouldn't do that. Hit on a customer, I mean. That'd be rude."

Holy crap, Pandora thought. It was like taking her foot out of her mouth and shoving her ass in instead.

Thankfully, Caleb was sticking with his brooding silence.

Wincing, she glanced at Tobias, who still looked amused. With an actual reason this time.

"I'll let the two of you do lunch, then," the older man decided. He glanced through the beaded doorway. Pandora followed his gaze and cringed. How'd the crowd get even bigger?

She couldn't make Tobias go out there. They'd be on him like a pack of rabid dogs. And yes, she eyed the older man, noting the freakishly calm stance and lack of anger emanating off him, he could probably handle himself fine. Better than she could, that was for sure.

Still…

"Tobias, did you want to—"

Before she could finish the sentence, Caleb snapped to attention, straightening from the wall like a stiff board. Nice to know he could get stiff that fast; she almost smirked. Then she saw the intense anger in his eyes and swallowed.

What? Did he think she was going to invite his dad to stay?

"It's a little crowded with shoppers in the store now," she finished slowly, choosing her words as if they would guide her through a live minefield. "So, um, would you like to go out the back and cut across the alley to your own shop?"

Tobias rocked back on his heels, mimicking his son's stance and considered the two of them. He glanced through the beads again and then arched a brow at Caleb.

Clueless, Pandora looked at the younger man, too, trying to figure out what the silent question was that had just been asked. But she couldn't read a thing on either man's face.

She wanted to scream. Even if it wasn't a talent, she'd at least had a decent grasp of reading body language—bs, that was. Before Sean. Now? She might as well be blind.

She eyed the two men and their stoic faces and apparently relaxed stance. They came across as totally mellow strangers.

And the hair on the back of her neck was standing up due to all the antagonism flying through the room.

It was frustrating the hell out of her.

"Thanks, Pandora," Tobias accepted. Then he flashed her a charming smile. "And is there any chance I could get a piece of that cake to go? I was too full after lunch, but it'd be a nice snack later."

Pandora bit her lip, not sure why she felt as if she needed to stick around and protect Caleb. The man obviously didn't need little ole her standing in front of him.

But still…

"I'd appreciate it," Tobias prodded.

Unable to do otherwise, Pandora nodded and hurried into the tiny kitchen at the far end of the sunroom. She cut a fat slab of cake and scooped it into a cardboard box, not bothering to lick the decadent ganache off her knuckle as she pressed the lid down and rushed back out.

Neither man had moved. From what she could tell, neither had said a word, either.

"Here you go," she said, staying by the kitchen and its door to the alley, instead of taking the cake over to Tobias. "I hope you enjoy it. It's my favorite recipe."

Tobias gave his son a nod, then strode toward Pandora. A goodbye? Or acknowledgment that Caleb had won this round? Pandora wasn't sure which.

Caleb, of course, just stood there. Did nothing rile the guy?

"I do appreciate your hospitality," Tobias said as he reached her. "For the cake, and for making my son feel welcome. I'm sure one bite of your delicious offerings and he'll be ready to stay in Black Oak and enjoy himself for a while."

"Um, you're welcome?" Pandora murmured. She wanted to point out that as delicious as chocolate was, it wasn't magic cake. He was asking for an awful lot from a lunch that she wasn't even sure Caleb would eat.

Without another word to her, or to his son, Tobias gave a jaunty wave and headed out the back door. Pandora plaited her fingers together, staring in the direction Tobias had gone until she heard the door close. She shifted her gaze to the café tables then, noting that half needed tidying.

Her gaze landed everywhere but on Caleb.

Murmurs rose from the store. She turned, grateful that something might demand her attention.

Then she winced. She could almost feel the barbs of fury shooting at her from the disappointed crowd. They'd obviously thought the show would move into the store, where they could get a better view. They'd probably positioned themselves to best greet, and grill, Tobias as he left the café. And she'd ruined it.

But she didn't hear the chimes over the front door ring at all, which meant they were still circling, waiting for fresh meat. Or in this case, a hunk named Caleb.

They could just keep waiting. And, hopefully, purchasing. After all, she was apparently giving away cake back here.

Speaking of…

"Would you like something to eat?" she asked, finally looking directly at Caleb.

Under his slash of black brows, his eyes were intense as he inspected her. His expression didn't change as his gaze traveled from her face, then skimmed down her body in a way that made her wish she was wearing one of those loose, New Agey dresses Fifi and Cassiopeia wore.

Or that she was naked.

Either one would be better than this feeling that there wasn't a chance in hell she could measure up to the sexual challenge Caleb presented.

A sexual challenge she wasn't even positive he was issuing. For all she knew, the guy gave that same hot but unreadable look to his mail lady when she asked him to sign for delivery.

Her body on fire, her mind a mess of tangled thoughts, she gave in to the desire to run.

"I'll be right back," she muttered as she hurried back to the small kitchen again. This time, instead of hacking through the cake and throwing it in a container, she carefully selected a plate, cut a precise slice and centered it on the cobalt glass plate. She retrieved a can of whipped cream and sprayed a sweet little rosette of white on top of the chocolate.

This was crazy. It wasn't as though the guy was going to ask her on a date. He was here to… What? Shop for Christmas gifts? Score an aphrodisiac-laced lunch?

Pandora groaned. Oh, wouldn't that be sweet? Insane, impossible and inconceivable—but so sweet to have sex with a man like Caleb Black. A man who, with just one look, could make her body go lax, her legs quiver and her nipples beg in pouty supplication.

But Caleb Black was the kind of guy who went for powerful women. A woman who could hold her own, who would demand he fulfill her every fantasy and in doing so, would show him things he hadn't even dreamed of yet.

In other words, totally not Pandora.

Except…she wanted him for herself.

She grabbed two forks, setting one neatly on the plate. With the other she stabbed a huge chunk from the cake still on the serving dish. Shoving it in her mouth, she closed her eyes and, with a sigh, let the chocolate work its way through her system. Calming, centering, soothing.

God, she loved chocolate.

More than sex, she insisted to herself. Which was a lie, of course, but with a little work she might start believing it. After all, chocolate's only threat was to her hips.

Swallowing hard as she imagined what kind of threat

Caleb might pose to her body, she scooped up the plate and forced herself to return to the café.

"You look like that visit barely registered on your stress meter, but mine is off the charts. Nothing pulls me out of the dumps like chocolate, so I figured you might want some," she said with a sheepish smile as she set the cake on a nearby table. Glancing through the beads at the nosy crowd, she sighed, then sat opposite the plate and waited.

"Why's it empty in here?" he asked, his voice as surly as his scowl. But hey, words were words. Who was she to quibble over tone?

"The café closes at two. We still have shoppers in the store, but Fifi is helping them. People know we're closed. They won't come back here," she assured him. "It's not much, but at least it's a tiny semblance of privacy."

He gave her a look, those gold eyes dark. She could see the anger in them now, as clearly as she could see it in the set of his chin and his clenched fists. But now she could see hurt, too, in the way he hunched his shoulders, the droop of his lips.

"I guess this isn't a surprise visit for the holidays," she said with a tentative smile, wishing he'd smile again.

"Prodigal son, didn't Tobias say?"

"You call your father by his name?" Why was she so shocked? It wasn't as if he was the kind of guy to call his old man daddy.

He shrugged, staring at the door to the alley. Finally, he came over and sat across from her. She didn't know if it was because she'd worn him down with her inane chatter or if he was emotionally exhausted from the confrontation. It definitely wasn't because he was suddenly in the mood to be friendly. Not the way he was glowering. The frown didn't detract from his mouth.

A deliciously sensual mouth, she noticed. She licked her

own lips, wondering what he tasted like. How he kissed. Whether he was slow and sensual or if he liked it wild and intense.

"You interested in providing a little prodigal entertainment?"

"Hmm?"

She'd bet he was a wild kind of guy. One who'd take her mouth in a hard, mind-blowing kiss and leave her begging for a taste of his promised sexual nirvana.

"Yeah, you're interested."

Pandora ripped her gaze off his mouth to meet his eyes in horror. Was she that obvious? Was she so unskilled that she couldn't even hide her should-be-secret lusty thoughts?

What the hell was she doing? The man was off-limits. He was bad news, with a capital H heartbreak. And while she was intrigued enough to risk her heart, she still had the bruises from risking her reputation and ego.

"No, sorry. I'm not interested, I'm just curious."

"Curious?" His smile was pure temptation. Wicked and knowing. He didn't push, though. Instead, he cocked a brow at the slice of cake she'd set on the table between them, then pulled it toward him. He pressed his finger on a crumb and lifted it to his mouth.

Pandora swore her thighs melted. Heat, intense and needy, clawed through her good intentions.

PUZZLED, CALEB STUDIED the woman in front of him.

He'd got what he wanted out of this visit—to see the back room and access to the bike shop. Her interest would be easy to use to get back in, anytime he wanted.

But could he do it?

Seated at the table like a dainty lady about to serve some fancy-ass tea, Pandora looked as calm as a placid lake. Except for those occasional flashes of hunger he saw in her pretty eyes. With her smooth, dark red hair and porcelain complexion, she looked like the special china doll his sister had as a kid. If he remembered correctly, he'd broken that doll at one point or another.

Something to keep in mind.

He noted the lush fullness of her lips and the sweet curve of her breasts beneath the white silky fabric of her conservatively cut blouse. His body stirred in reluctant interest. Good girls weren't his thing, but his body wasn't paying much attention to that detail.

"Were you going to try the cake?" Pandora prodded, looking a little put out at his inspection. She sounded as if she wanted to say something—probably something rude—but good girls didn't do things like that.

He grinned. Yet another reason not to be good.

He had questions, so more to pacify her than because he wanted any, he swiped his finger over the frosted cake and sucked the sweet confection while holding her gaze.

Her eyes narrowed. He imagined she was trying to look stern, but came off as cute instead. Her store location was handy, she probably had an inside track to the town and townspeople, and she looked as if she was one of those crazy trust-until-proved-untrustworthy kind of people.

A much better cover than the loosey-goosey vamp who'd hit on him before. She was going to be easier to, well, manipulate.

"I remember this store now," he mused as he looked, noting the deep purple walls with garlands of flowers, stars, suns and moons painted along the ceiling. "I broke in here one night on a dare, hoping to see a rumored séance. It wasn't a restaurant then, though."

"Broke in? I always heard that you were wild, but I thought those rumors were exaggerated."

He just shrugged. It wasn't as though it was a secret that

he'd been well on his way to a life of crime in his teen years. Hell, he considered it early training for his undercover assignments.

The frosting was good. Ready for more, he took the fork and scooped up a big bite.

"This room used to be set up for classes and readings," she explained, still frowning at him in a chiding sort of way. "My mother started using it for storage when the mayor changed the permit requirements to demand a twenty percent kickback."

Caleb snorted. He'd grown up the son of an infamous con artist and spent his adult years dealing with criminal dregs. But he was pretty sure politics were the biggest scam around.

"Gotta hand it to her. The mayor's big on clever ways to line the town coffers."

She gave him a narrow-eyed look at odds with his sweet, goody-goody image of her. "Isn't Mayor Parker your aunt?"

Realizing he was starving, he forked up more of the rich cake and grinned. "Yep."

"So this is like old home week. Will you be staying with your aunt instead of your father?"

"Nope. I'm at the Black Oak Inn. Room seventeen, if you're out wandering later," he said with a wink.

Her eyes rounded. She caught her breath as if grabbing back a response that scared her. The move made her cotton top slide temptingly over rounded breasts. He watched as her nipples beaded against the fabric. Suddenly starving, he wanted nothing more than to lean across the table and taste her.

Her reaction was gratifying. His own irritated him, though. She wasn't his type, and given the situation, she was off-limits. He just had to remember that.

"I'm sure I'll see her, though. Want me to talk her into dropping those fees for you?" he offered with another wink.

"I don't do readings."

That sounded bitter. His chewing slowed; he gave her a searching look.

She gave a tiny shrug and looked away.

Off-limits? A part of him wanted to push. To ask questions and get to know her better. The rest of him, the burned-out, disenchanted, cynical DEA-trained part of him, said that unless it pertained to the case, it didn't matter.

Since he wasn't sticking around longer than it took to clear his old man, the cynic got to call the shots.

"So what's the deal?" Caleb asked instead. "You seem to know Tobias pretty well, right?"

"I wouldn't say I know your father well," she mused, her eyes skimming toward the alley. "No more so than anyone else in town. I mean, he's the patriarch, isn't he? From what I understand, he's got more power than the mayor and the sheriff combined. People look up to him, turn to him for advice. I've been hearing accolades since the day I arrived."

"You're not a native of Black Oak?" Why had he thought she was?

"I am native," she said, drawing the words out. "I think I was even in a few classes with your sister, Maya. But I left for college and haven't been back much since."

"So why'd you get a job here? You're interested in this New Age stuff?"

She looked toward the dangling beaded doorway with shelves of crystal balls lining either side and rolled her eyes.

"Interested? I don't know about that. More like indoctrinated." At his arched brow, she shrugged and admitted, "Cassiopeia is my mother."

He might only have a vague recollection of the store, but he definitely remembered Cassiopeia. Third-generation woo-woo queen, all the guys in high school had had crushes on her. Bodacious, outrageous and eccentric, the outgoing redhead had a scary handle on that psychic stuff she sold to her customers.

"I remember your mom. She did readings at my senior carnival."

"Mine, too." Pandora didn't sound nearly as intrigued as he'd been. The son of a colorful character, Caleb could sympathize.

Talk about the apple falling so far from the tree it could make orange juice. Now that he knew what to look for, he could see the resemblance in the curve of her cheeks, the rounded eyes more hazel than her mother's emerald. And, of course, the red hair, again, more muted in Pandora's case. It was as if she'd stepped into a shadow instead of embracing the full wattage her mother liked to wave around.

Interesting.

Even more interesting was that Caleb was finding muted about the sexiest thing he'd ever encountered. He just couldn't figure out why since he'd always been a Technicolor kind of guy.

"You know what I heard while we were still in the store, then again while you were in the back getting cake?"

"You mean while you were hiding back here?" she corrected.

Caleb grinned, glad to see she had claws. It was always more fun to tangle with a wildcat than a pussycat.

"I heard people saying you serve up something besides food back here."

This time the color wasn't subtle. Nope, she blushed a hot, brilliant red. Her eyes flew to the store, then to the cake before meeting his gaze. A stubborn line furrowed between her brows.

"I have no idea what you're talking about," she dismissed.

"You're a horrible liar."

"A gentleman would take the hint and change the subject."

"Sweetie, I've never worried about being a gentleman."

"Obviously."

Grinning, Caleb decided it was time to change gears. He stood, and with a glance at the still-milling crowd in the store, decided to take his cue from his father and head out the back way.

"Walk me out?" he said, making the demand sound like a request.

"The back? The door's right there," she pointed out. But she got to her feet anyway.

Caleb didn't know why he was pushing it. He'd already declared her off-limits, and while he was a guy who was all about pushing boundaries, he never crossed lines he, himself, drew.

But right now, he didn't care.

"So is it true?" he asked, heading toward the door, counting on her being trapped by good manners into following.

"Is what true?"

"Do you really serve aphrodisiacs?"

She ground to a halt so fast, she teetered in her flat-heeled boots. "Don't believe everything you hear," she said dismissively.

"So, it's a lie?"

"It's more of an…exaggeration," she decided. "After all, who's to say whether aphrodisiacs are real or whether they're a figment of the imagination?"

"I have a really good imagination." He reached out and took her hand, lifting it to his mouth.

"What are you doing?" she asked with a gasp, tugging. But he didn't let go.

"You have chocolate," he told her, "just…here."

He swiped his tongue over her knuckle. Her eyes went heated, her breath shuddered and she leaned against the wall with the cutest little mewling noise.

In an instant, Caleb went from amused to rock-hard. An overwhelming urge to touch her, to taste her, washed over him.

Never a man to ignore his gut, he went with the feeling. Stepping forward, the rich taste of chocolate still on his lips, Caleb pressed her body between his and the chilly glass. One hand on either side of her head, he leaned closer.

"This is crazy," she breathed, twisting her hands together at her waist. But she didn't pull away. Instead, she lifted her chin.

That's all the encouragement he needed.

Holding her gaze captive, he brushed his lips over her soft, sweetly moist mouth. He slid his tongue along her lower lip, then gently nibbled at the cushioned flesh.

Passion throbbed, urging him to take it deeper, to go faster. But he resisted.

For the first time in forever, Caleb felt as if he'd come home. Even as the sexual heat zinged through his body like lightning, he relaxed. Need pounded through him, making him ache. But he was at peace.

It was that confusion more than any desire to stop that had him pulling back. He stared, waiting for Pandora to open her eyes. In them he saw confusion, hunger and a hint of fear.

The same as he was feeling.

"You might want to go easy on that cake," he suggested, brushing his knuckles over her cheek before forcing himself away. Stepping back from the warm, soft curves of her body was harder than it should have been. Way too freaking hard. Caleb frowned, not sure what the hell was going on here.

Hand on the doorknob, he looked back. She was still leaning against the wall, her breath ragged and her eyes huge.

"Like I said, I'm in room seventeen. Come on by if you want to do something about that interest. Or serve up something a little hotter than cake."

4

"I'LL HAVE THE PASTA SPECIAL, the house salad with raspberry vinaigrette and the house white," Kathy ordered over the melodic jingle of crystal and silver.

"And you, madam? What would you like?"

"I'd like what's in room seventeen," Pandora muttered, staring blindly at the menu.

"Beg your pardon?"

"What's in room seventeen?" Kathy prodded with a nudge of her toe under the white linen-covered table.

Playing back what she'd said, Pandora scrunched her nose in a rueful grimace. God, she couldn't get Caleb Black out of her head. His intense gold eyes, his sexy swagger and oh, baby, those magic lips.

He'd tasted so good. So enticing. Like the most deliciously decadent chocolate éclair. Rich and tempting and mouth-wateringly hedonistic. All she had to do was close her eyes and she could relive the sweet slide of his mouth over hers, her body heating instantly at the memory.

"Dory?"

Pandora blinked. Damn, she'd done it again. Spaced off into Caleb fantasyland. She'd been taking that trip over and over and over for the past two days. She'd just bet his body was a wild amusement park, too. One she was in desperate danger of knocking on the door of room seventeen to beg to ride.

"Pandora!"

Pandora winced and gave the waiter an apologetic smile and said, "Sorry, I'll have the same thing."

Not that she had any idea what Kathy had ordered.

Clearly clued in to big news by Pandora's dinginess, Kathy leaned forward on both elbows and demanded with her usual rapid-fire pace, "What's going on? You've got news, don't you? How's the store doing? Have you put your stamp on it? Do you love the café angle? Are people doing the deed on the tables thanks to that menu we came up with?"

Pandora's fingers tapped a rhythm on the table as she pondered.

"Well?" Kathy used one perfectly manicured finger to poke Pandora in the arm.

"I was waiting to see if you had more questions," she replied with a wicked grin.

"Cute. Now spill."

She'd called Kathy to meet her for lunch for just this reason, to spill the dirty deets about Caleb Black and his hot lips. Her friend was the only person she could tell, because not only was Kathy a great sounding board, she was sane. She'd be the voice of reason and keep Pandora from doing something insanely stupid, like chasing a man who was totally wrong for her. But she'd also keep Pandora from chickening out if her idea—and Caleb—were actually doable.

But now that the moment of truth was here, she couldn't quite share. Wasn't sure she was ready for this kind of risk. So she sidestepped.

"The store is actually doing well. There's a ton of business. The new café is bringing in lots of customers. They're shopping in the store, heck, even the online storefront is getting a lot more traffic. Sales are up forty percent over this time last year and I've banked almost enough to cover the quarterly tax payment."

Pressing her lips tight to stop the bragging, Pandora waited for a reaction. She was a little embarrassed at how proud she was of the store. Even more embarrassed at how much she wanted people, any people—but especially people in Black Oak—to know she was kicking butt. To know that she wasn't a failure.

"Wow," Kathy said with a huge grin, clapping her hands together in delight. "I told you it would work. You're totally rocking the businesswoman gig. I'm excited for you."

"I wouldn't say rocking it," Pandora said, blushing a little. "But it is going so much better than I'd expected. I thought I was going to have to work a lot harder to convince people that oysters, strawberries and asparagus would make their love lives more exciting. But I barely had to advertise. Just opened the café, showed the menu and once word got out, it's been packed."

"Beats little blue pills, right?"

Pandora laughed, leaning back in her chair and letting the soothing elegance of the restaurant wash over her.

"Oh, yeah, I have it on good authority that I'm way ahead of the little blue pill," she agreed with a grin. "Do you know how much I now know about sexual aids for the elderly? I mean, yes, the customers are all ages, but it's the elderly that want to share."

Pandora paused while the waiter set a basket of sourdough bread and a dish of roasted garlic and olive tapenade on the table. As soon as he left, she continued.

"They are so grateful and excited about the aphrodisiacs— and to give them credit, about a place to get killer desserts— that they seem to have a need to fill me in on their newfound vigor, enthusiasm, length…. It's TMI run amok."

Kathy choked on her wine. "Length?"

Pandora's brow quirked, then as she realized what Kathy must be thinking, she giggled. "Eww, no. I meant how long their little trysts are lasting now. Apparently chocolate cake is accredited with an extra twenty minutes of good lovin'."

"And they never discovered the power of chocolate before?"

"Not naked."

This time it was Kathy who wrinkled her nose.

"It sounds like you've had plenty of entertainment. Leave it to Black Oak to stay lively."

"Yep, the town is chock-full of characters." Pandora hesitated, then took another fortifying sip of wine. "Including Tobias Black's kids. Do you remember them?"

"Ooooh, baby," Kathy said with a low-throated growl. "I had one memorable night with Gabriel right after graduation, remember? I still consider that my introduction to real pleasure, if you know what I mean."

Pandora winced. Maybe she really did have a sex-confessional sign floating over her head. Before Kathy could share details, she changed the subject. "Did you know the rest of his family?"

"Not so much. Maya is a little younger than we are, Caleb a few years older than Gabriel. Their mom died when they were really little and I think their aunt tried to get custody but Tobias wouldn't let them go. I remember my mom saying he might not have done them any favors since the boys ran pretty wild. He used to travel a lot, and sometimes he took the kids, but mostly they stayed home on their own." She frowned, sopping up oil with her bread before picking it apart in tiny little bites. "They had a few minor brushes with the law, teenage things, but nothing major. I remember they were scary smart in school, though. Like they didn't even have to study to ruin the curve, you know?"

Mulling this over, Pandora nodded.

"Why? Are you selling bed-y-bye snacks to old man Black? Now, *that's* a guy who's aged well. Talk about a hottie. I'd think he'd have little need for a chocolate-coated pick-me-up."

Mr. Black? A hottie? Pandora wasn't sure what to say to that. It wasn't that she didn't agree with Kathy, because Tobias Black was definitely a good-looking man. But it was kinda creepy thinking about him that way when she was nursing a serious case of the hots for his son.

"If he's as good a kisser as his son, I'm sure he doesn't," Pandora agreed, nibbling at her own piece of bread and nervously waiting for the reaction. Once upon a time, she'd have relied on her own ability to read a person, to gauge their body language, and had trusted her own judgment. But now? Now all she was sure of was that she couldn't be trusted.

The question was, did that mean she shouldn't trust her lust for Caleb? Or her fear of him?

Kathy gave a gratifying gasp, tossed what was left of her bread on her plate and leaned forward to grasp Pandora's arm. "Spill. All the details. Which brother, how was it, where'd you do it and were you naked?"

Pandora giggled.

"Caleb. It was amazing. In the café, and oh, my God, of course not."

"But you wanted to be?"

"Absolutely," she admitted with a sigh. Her smile softened as she remembered his lips again. The taste of him, male, hot and just a little chocolaty. Their bodies hadn't even touched, yet she'd been more turned on than the last time she'd had full-on, two-naked-bodies and real-live-orgasm sex.

More turned on than she'd ever been in her life, actually.

"In the café?" Kathy said, a naughty look dancing in her green eyes. "Had you shared one of those sexy treats?"

Pandora opened her mouth to say no, then closed it.

She hadn't put much thought into it, but he'd had a few big bites of the Foreplay cake. So had she, for that matter. But their lust had been the real deal. At least, hers had.

Doubt, always lurking somewhere but now painfully close to the surface thanks to Sean, reared its ugly head.

"A couple bites is all," she admitted with a frown. "But a lot of the power of an aphrodisiac is in the mind, isn't it? My grammy always said that most magics require belief to work. The power of suggestion and all that."

"Kinda like a low-cut dress, huh?"

Pandora grinned, acknowledging Kathy's point with a wave of her fork. "A little."

Then her smile fell away. "Do you think that's why he kissed me? Of course it is," she answered herself. "I mean, he just got to town, he's so gorgeous he probably has women throwing themselves at him. Why else would he kiss a perfect stranger?"

Why had she thought he'd found her special? That was crazy. She wasn't the type to inspire uncontrollable lust. Heck, she rarely inspired a second look.

Seeing where her mind was going, Kathy shook her head and gave Pandora's forearm a chiding tap. "Stop that. You're counting yourself out before you even consider the situation."

"What's to consider?"

"The details, of course. Start at the beginning."

Pandora arched one brow. "When the dinosaurs roamed? Or back further than that?"

"Smart-ass. When did you first meet Caleb Black?"

Pandora picked at her slice of bread again, wishing she'd never brought the subject up. For just a while there she'd been riding high on the idea that a man so sexy he made her toes curl had been attracted enough for a kiss at first sight. But now? Now she figured she should raise the prices in the café, since her aphrodisiacs were that strong.

"Deets," Kathy prodded. "Has he been in town long? When was the kiss?"

"Two days ago," she finally confessed. "He came into the store. There was this big confrontation between him and his dad, then I gave him a piece of cake and he kissed me."

Just remembering gave her shivers. It'd been so incredible. For a guy who came across as a total hard-ass, his lips had been so, so soft.

She took a shaky breath and brushed the bread crumbs off her fingers.

Maybe the why didn't matter. She'd had an incredible kiss. Wasn't that what counted?

"Wow, talk about a lot going on. I'll want the details of all the rest later. But for now, how was the kiss?" Kathy asked, her eyes huge. "Was it amazing?"

"It was…special," she decided with a soft smile.

"Uh-oh."

"What uh-oh?" Pandora saw the concerned look in Kathy's eyes and shook her head. "No. No uh-oh. I'm not getting romantic ideas. That'd be crazy, considering he only kissed me because of the cake. I'm just saying, it was a hot kiss that didn't follow the standard moves, you know?"

"Standard moves?"

"Yeah. You know how usually the first kiss with a guy is more about the anticipation and, well, introduction to his style?"

Kathy nodded.

"There was no anticipation because, I mean, who the hell kisses a complete stranger in a café while sneaking out the back door?" Kathy's brows creased, but before she could ask, Pandora continued, "And he wasn't so much introducing his style as he was…"

"Was…what?"

"Making me melt?" Pandora admitted with a helpless little laugh. "Honestly, I have no idea why he kissed me. I just know that it was amazing."

"Once again, uh-oh," Kathy worried, apprehension clear in her eyes.

"What?"

"Be careful. Those Black men are heartbreakers. They went through girls like crazy. They always left them smiling, sure. But they never stuck around. Still, you don't need that," Kathy warned.

"I know he's off-limits," Pandora said with a bad-tempered shrug. "I didn't say I was crazy enough to think one flirty little kiss—especially one that didn't include tongue—means I'm in for some hot and wild bad-boy sex."

"He's not off-limits. He's just trouble. But if all you're thinking about is getting naked and doing the horizontal tango, then maybe you should. Just as long as you're clear from the start that it's just sex. Nothing more."

Caleb Black. Naked. Oh, man, she'd bet he was deliciously built. Those wide shoulders would have the kind of muscles she could cling to as he moved in her, his long torso and slender hips arched over her straining body. She knew he had a sweet little hiney, but it'd look even better bare than it had covered in denim. She'd bet it was firm, so hard she'd barely make a dent if her fingers gripped it. Heat washed over Pandora so fast she had to take a sip of her wine before she combusted.

"That is all you're thinking about, isn't it?" Kathy prodded.

"Well, now I'm thinking about Caleb naked and can't remember your question," Pandora said with a pout.

"You're only looking for sex, right? Not a relationship?

Not a wild time that might turn into something special once he realizes how great you are?"

"No," she protested vehemently. This was a stupid conversation. All she'd wanted was to share her little bit of sexy news and suddenly she was defending a fling with a guy who probably kissed every woman he met. That didn't mean he had any interest in actually getting naked and slippery. "I'm not going to do anything stupid. I'd have to be crazy to fall for a guy like Caleb Black. I'm not his type and that kiss was probably the last contact we'll ever have."

Kathy leaned back in the booth and gave her a long, searching look. After a few seconds, Pandora squirmed. She didn't like people looking that close, or that deep.

"Okay, I've changed my mind. I think you should go for it."

"Go for what? It wasn't like an invitation to a relationship. It was more like a hit-and-run."

"Maybe. But maybe not. I'm just saying if he hits again, you should take him up on a little ride. I'll bet he's the kind of guy who'll make you see stars."

Stars. Pandora wasn't a virginal prude. She liked sex. Especially if it was good sex. She read the how-to articles in women's magazines and erotic books, she knew her body and wasn't shy about giving directions when necessary.

But, typically, the guys she'd been with weren't big on directions.

Which was probably why she'd never seen stars. With Sean, she'd seen a flicker or two but never full-oh-my-God stars.

"So?" Kathy prodded.

"So what?"

"So, are you going to shoot for the stars? Or are you going to take the route of avoidance?"

Avoidance. All the way.

After all, the last time she'd given in to a sexy fling, she'd paid. Big-time. And Sean hadn't been anywhere near as hot, gorgeous or tempting as Caleb. Getting involved with him was crazy.

The last thing she needed was to get herself all upside down over a guy. Even a just-sex-and-nothing-more kind of guy. A more confident woman might be able to handle a sweet fling with someone like that, but her? She wasn't that kind of woman.

For once, though, she wanted to be. She wanted to have a purely sexual fling based on nothing more than physical satisfaction and excitement. She wanted to be exciting and dynamic. Fun and maybe a little wild. No expectations of anything long-term or emotional.

And maybe, just maybe, to relax knowing that because she didn't expect anything, her inability to read him couldn't be termed a failure.

"He's not going to ask me out," she said again.

"So why don't you ask him out?"

Why didn't she jump up on the table and strip naked while singing Katy Perry's "Hot N Cold"? "I can't do that," she excused.

Kathy just gave her The Look.

Pandora pressed a hand to her stomach, feeling as if she was about to jump off a very high cliff.

It was scary.

But it was also exciting as hell.

"I'm not promising anything. But—and it's a teensy-tiny but—but…if I do, and if he says yes, then our next kiss *will* involve tongues," she vowed.

CALEB LEANED HIS LEATHER-CLAD shoulder against the black iron lamppost and stared across the street at the warm welcome of Moonspun Dreams.

He'd promised Hunter he'd give it two weeks. So in between watching the store, he'd spent the past four days nosing around. He'd hit what passed for the party scene in Black Oak. Bounced through a few bars, made himself known to the major partiers and netted a couple easy introductions to the town's lower-level drug dealers. The first step was to get the lay of the land, to gauge how challenging the bust would be and to establish his identity.

The ecstasy was definitely available and at discounts usually only seen in Black Friday sales ads. Marketing 101, make the product cheap and plentiful until you'd hooked enough suckers, then bleed them dry. As he would on any DEA job, he'd scored a little from each dealer, sending it all to Hunter for analysis. But experience and instinct told him it was all coming from the same source. A source nobody could—or would—pinpoint.

So far this visit was a bust. He hadn't found out much for Hunter. He hadn't cleared his father. Of course, he'd done his damnedest to avoid seeing his father at all after that first surprise visit, but that was neither here nor there.

And all he could think about was that one small kiss from the intriguingly reticent Pandora.

Unlike his usual M.O. in breaking a drug ring, this time he had no cover. Around here, everyone and their granny knew who he was. Many had pinched his cheeks at the same time they'd bemoaned his probable criminal career. That all worked in his favor, his lousy rep ensuring that nobody questioned his activities.

Still, that was then. He'd have liked to come home and be appreciated for who he really was now. An upright citizen who'd made a life outside of crime.

Except, he realized with a tired sigh, that he really didn't have any life outside of crime. Which was why he'd quit.

To relax, to get a hobby and to figure out what he wanted from life.

Which brought his thoughts back, yet again, to Pandora. He couldn't figure out why the woman fascinated him, but she did. She was quiet, when he usually went for the flamboyant. She seemed sweet, which he was pretty sure he was allergic to. And she was friendly with his father, which meant she had questionable taste.

As he pondered, and yes, stared at Moonspun's window hoping to catch a glimpse of the sexy Ms. Easton, something on the corner across the street caught his eye. Two guys in black hoodies, both hunched over as if they were trying to blend in with the brick siding of Pandora's building. Caleb shook his head in disgust. He didn't need years of DEA experience to recognize a drug deal going down. Hell, the little old lady walking her Pomeranian was shooting the two guys the same disgusted look. When one of the guys made a hulking gesture toward her, obviously trying to intimidate, she flipped him the bird and kept mincing along in her fluffy pink knitted hat. Caleb could see the goon growl from across the street. He made as if to go after her, when his buddy grabbed his arm, saying something and showing him a bag of what Caleb assumed were the drugs in question.

Hulk flexed a little, then followed the Baggie into the alley. Caleb considered trailing them. He had no jurisdiction. Hell, he was on a pseudovacation with his resignation sitting on his boss's desk. It was the *pseudo* part of that equation that made him hesitate, not the vacation or the resignation.

But, really, how far did fake authority go? Favors for buddies and an unexplained need to vindicate his father didn't give him the jurisdiction to bust a deal going down.

Then again, when had he ever worried about rules?

Before he could step off the curb, though, Hulk slunk out

of the alley. His hoodie pulled low so his face was shadowed, he loped down the street.

No point following the doper. Caleb wanted the guy hooked into whoever was running the game. He waited for him to come out.

But the alley opening stayed empty.

Five minutes later, Caleb was mentally cussing and ready to hit something. There were only two businesses accessible through that alley. Moonspun Dreams and his dad's bike shop.

Dammit.

Before he could decide how he wanted to handle it, a car pulled up next to him. Caleb's sigh was infinitesimal as he cut his gaze to the sheriff's cruiser. His eyes were the only thing he moved, though.

Because he knew damn well the lack of reaction would piss Jeff off.

"I heard you were back in town," Jeff Kendall, the bane of Caleb's high school years, said as he unfolded himself from his car, leaning his forearms on the open door and offering an assessing look.

"Looks like you heard right."

"C'mon, Black. Just because we didn't get along before doesn't mean you should be holding a grudge," Kendall said with his good-ole-boy smile. The one he'd perfected in grade school, usually used in tandem with tattling to the teacher about the bad Black kids.

It still made Caleb want to punch him.

Hunter had broached the possibility of bringing in local law enforcement, but Caleb had nixed the idea. If the locals knew about the drugs and hadn't shut them down, they might be dirty. And that'd been before he knew who he'd be dealing with. When he'd heard that this guy was in charge of the law in town, Caleb had sneered. No wonder they had problems.

"Look, I'm just offering a welcome home, okay. I hear you've seen your share of trouble after leaving town. I'm not here to add to it. But if you don't mind a friendly warning, keep it clean while you're enjoying Christmas with your dad."

Caleb didn't even blink. After all, that was his cover. Prodigal loser back for the holidays, nothing to his name except a bad attitude and a crappy reputation. And, of course, a whole lot of family baggage.

All in all, it was pretty damn close to the truth.

His silent stare seemed to bug Kendall, though. The guy shifted from foot to foot, then frowned.

"Are you standing here for a reason?" the sheriff prodded.

"Just biding my time."

Kendall glanced around, his gaze lighting on Moonspun Dreams, then flashing back to Caleb. "Looking for a little help in the sack, are you?"

Caleb didn't move. Didn't bat an eyelash. But his entire being snapped to attention.

"Thanks to Pandora and her little concoctions," the sheriff continued, "Black Oak is seeing more sex than a teenager with his daddy's credit card and a link to online porn."

"Geez, Kendall. Can't you score your own credit card yet?"

The sheriff glared, then jerked his head toward the store again. "You must be in the market for a little bedroom boost. There's nothing else in there for you."

It took a second before that sunk in. Caleb's grin was just this side of a smirk as he raised his brows to the other man. "You warning me off?"

"I'm just saying you need to watch your step." Kendall rested one hand on the gun at his hip and tilted his head. "This isn't your town. It's mine. Crime is low and trouble is rare. I'm not going to like it if you sweep in here, stir up a bunch of problems, then make me kick you out."

Low crime and rare trouble? Was the guy really that bad at his job? Caleb's eyes slashed to the corner where the drug deal had gone down. Good thing Hunter had sent him here, since Kendall clearly had no clue what was going on.

"Do you watch John Wayne movies on your nights off and practice that shit in front of the mirror?" was all he said, though.

Kendall's red face tightened, right along with his fist. "I'm a sworn officer of the law. That makes me in charge of this town, Black. So watch your ass."

The guy's delusional self-importance amused Caleb enough that he could easily ignore the jabs.

Besides, he was pretty sure he'd just seen the first break in this case. And he'd much rather follow that up than exchange insults with this dipwad.

"Tell you what. You've piqued my interest," Caleb said, straightening for the first time and stepping toward the curb. "I'll head on over and see if the lady's interested in fielding a hit or two."

"I warned you, Black—"

Caleb just grinned and offered a jaunty salute before crossing the street.

The only thing better than having an excuse to flirt with Pandora handed to him on a silver platter was knowing how much it pissed Jeff the jerk off.

He was still grinning when he walked through the heavy brass door of Moonspun Dreams. Not seeing Pandora among the dozen or so people milling about the store, he made his way toward the back.

"The café is closed," the airy blonde said, tearing herself away from a shaggy-haired guy by the counter.

"I'm here to see Pandora."

"Oh." Her look was speculative, but she just shrugged and went back to helping her client.

Caleb swept the beads aside and stepped through the door. Then he almost tripped over his own size thirteens.

And grinned at the sight before him.

Holiday music playing loud enough to inspire a little swing of the hips as she arranged a bunch of green Christmas stuff, glittery bows and… Caleb squinted, were those blown-glass suns and moons…? Pandora stood at the top of a tall ladder before the wall by the door to the kitchen.

Her arms stretched high, her purple sweater pulled away from her jeans, showing off the pale silkiness of the small of her back. His gaze traced the tight fit of the denim, noting the hint, maybe, of a tattoo on her left hip.

Nah. She wasn't the tattoo type. She was the good-girl type.

Wasn't she?

Damned if he wasn't tempted to find out.

Whichever she was, she was one sweet sight.

Caleb's grin turned contemplative as he studied the curve of her butt, noting how perfectly those hips would fit in his hands.

A man who rarely tempered his impulses outside of work, Caleb figured why not find out. He glanced around, noting that there weren't any customers, or drug dealers, lurking about. Striding forward, he stepped behind the counter and planted a hand on either side of the ladder.

Just in time for Pandora's descent.

One step down, and her butt was level with his face. Right there within nibbling distance. Another step and he could push aside that nubby purple sweater and slide his lips along the small of her back. One more and, oh, yeah, baby…

Pandora gasped, her head swiveling to give him a wide-eyed look of shock.

"What the…?"

"Hi," he said, his voice low with more desire than he should be feeling for a woman he hadn't even groped yet.

A woman who was staring at him as if he was a combination of the Grinch and the Ghost of Christmas Future. The one who pushed poor Scrooge McDuck into his grave. In other words, she looked just as thrilled as dipwad Kendall had.

He shouldn't tease her. She was obviously on the shy and quiet side. Caleb didn't bother to move, though.

"What are you…? I mean, why…?" She stopped, closed her eyes and took a deep breath, then opened those hazel eyes again and offered a stiff smile. "What are you doing?"

"Making sure you don't fall off the ladder."

She looked down at the five inches between her feet and the ground, then met his gaze again with an arched brow. She had a little more makeup on today than she had earlier in the week. Something was smudged around her eyes, darkening those lush lashes. Her lips, though, those soft, soft lips, were temptingly bare.

"Aren't you the hero."

Caleb barked out a laugh. So much for shy and quiet. He'd expected her to get a little huffy. But no, she was a lot more fun than that.

And then she blew his mind. She slowly turned on the ladder, her hip brushing against his chest as she did. Awareness spiked through his body, hot and needy.

She licked her lips, the sensual move at odds with the nerves shimmering in her golden-green eyes. And she stepped down. They were so close, the tips of her breasts skimmed, just barely, a path down his chest, leaving behind a fiery trail.

Caleb's smile slowly faded.

He'd pegged Pandora as a sweet, small-town girl, maybe

a bit naive but with an open, curious mind. He'd figured on having a little fun flirting while he gathered info.

He definitely hadn't counted on a hard-on within the first three minutes of seeing her again.

Had he underestimated the sweet Pandora?

"Are you looking for a hero?" he asked, mentally rolling his eyes. At the question, because wasn't that what all women were looking for? A mythical guy to sweep them away and make all their dreams come true? And at the idea of *him* being hero material.

"Nah, I'd rather take care of things myself," she said with a smile and a tiny shrug. Her shoulder brushed against his wrist. "The term *hero* always makes me think of perfection. Since I can't live up to it, why would I want to have to deal with it?"

"So… What? You're looking for an antihero?" he joked, his gaze wandering over the soft, round curve of her face, noting the tiniest of dimples just there, to the left of her mouth.

"More like I'm not looking for anything," she said.

Yeah, right.

He looked closer, noting the stubborn set of her chin and the hint of anger in her eyes. Something, or someone, had burned her. Which meant she might be serious. A not-anything relationship, short and sweet, was right up his alley.

Besides, she had info he needed.

"You might not be looking for a hero, but from what I hear, you're exactly what I'm looking for," he told her.

"And what do you hear?" she asked, leaning back against the ladder, apparently not bothered at all that he was still holding her there, trapped by his arms. He didn't know if he liked that. He was used to making women nervous.

So he leaned in a little closer. Close enough that the scent of her perfume wrapped around him like a sensual fog. Close enough to see her heart beating a fast tattoo against the silky flesh at the base of her throat. Close enough to feel the tempting heat of her body.

His voice husky with need, his grin just a little strained, he said, "Rumor has it you're the lady to see if I'm looking for some really hot sex."

5

PANDORA'S MOUTH DROPPED, and with it all her bravado. Color washed, hot and wicked, over her cheeks as she blinked fast to try to clear her desire-blurred vision.

She stared at him, desperately trying to read him. Was this for real? Was he asking her for sex? Without even a bite of Foreplay cake or a nibble of an Orgasmic Oatmeal cookie? Did she say yes? Or ask him to wait until after her shift? The back room was empty, but still...

God, was she crazy? She gave herself a mental smack upside the head and tried to pull herself together. *Control, girl. Grab some control.*

But all she could think of was what he'd taste like naked and whether his chest was as tanned as his face under that tight black T-shirt.

Caleb's laughter washed over her, breaking the shocked spell. As soon as it did, color slid from her cheeks, leaving behind icy-cold humiliation.

"I guess that's what I get for listening to rumors," he said, still chortling. "Crazy, huh? That you'd be selling sex in here."

She frowned, his easy dismissal taking the edge off her embarrassment. What? He didn't think she could sell sex? He didn't think she was hot enough, wild enough, savvy enough? Was she so dismissible that he didn't think of sex after kissing her? Even now, when he had her trapped between his body and a ladder?

What the hell?

She'd put makeup on. She'd bought perfume, something sexy and inviting. She'd worn her tightest freaking jeans. And he dismissed her? Shoulders hunching, Pandora felt herself withdrawing. Pulling inside, where she could pretend it didn't hurt that, yet again, she didn't measure up. Or in this case, was so easily dismissible.

Here she'd spent the past three days in a state of horny anticipation, acting like a teenage girl wishing and wondering when her crush would reenter her sphere of existence. And what happened when he did?

He laughed at the idea of her and sex.

Before she could duck under his arm and scurry off, back to the obscurity of the kitchen or storage room, she caught sight of Bonnie the cat staring at her from the window seat with her pretty black-and-white head tilted to one side as if she was waiting for Pandora to find her spine.

The spine Sean had damaged with his lies, betrayal and oh-too-believable charm.

Then she thought of her vow to Kathy. Sure, it'd mostly been bravado, but still, she wanted to taste him. To feel his tongue on hers. To experience, at least one more time, hot and sexy Caleb kisses. She pressed her lips together, remembering. Then she squared her shoulders and gave him an arch look.

"Actually, most of Black Oak is thanking me daily for the effect I've had on their sex lives," she told him, lifting her chin.

His laughter trailed off, his smile slowly fading as a weird look came into his eyes. A chilly sort of calculation that made

Pandora, for the first time since he'd swaggered into her store four days ago, want to pull away from him.

He looked dangerous. And just a little scary.

"You don't say? Half the town, hmm? And why's that?"

"Aphrodisiacs, of course."

His gaze didn't change.

She shivered, this time letting herself duck under his arm and move away from the ladder. She needed some distance so she could reengage her brain. She made a show of petting Paulie, who was draped over a chair like a black, silky blanket. With a couple of feet between them, she watched Caleb turn, his leather-clad arms crossed over his chest as he leaned casually against the ladder.

"Aphrodisiacs?" he asked, his words as drawn out as his frown. "Like drugs?"

"What?" She yelped so loudly the mellowest cat in the world gave her a kitty frown before leaping in disapproval to the floor. Seriously shocked, Pandora gaped for a second before shaking her head. "No. Of course not. We're holistic here at Moonspun Dreams. The store, and my family, believes in herbal remedies. We even sell charts on acupressure pain relief instead of aspirin."

He kept staring as if he was measuring each word carefully. He didn't look happy, though. Pandora frowned. What? Was he looking for some kind of drug? She took in his long, shaggy hair, the hard look on his face and the black hoop piercing his ear. Her gaze skimmed over his beat-up leather jacket and the faded black T-shirt, down to the frayed hem of his jeans and his scuffed biker boots.

Sexy as hell? Check.

Bad boy personified? Double check.

A drug user?

She'd heard myriad rumors about those bad Black boys.

They were wild and untamed, they were trouble through and through. But she'd never heard even a whisper about drugs.

Her eyes skimmed that deliciously broad chest again, his muscles defined beneath the soft-looking fabric of his shirt. She looked into his vivid gold eyes, noting that they were shuttered but clear.

He looked as if he could and would beat anyone up, was hell on wheels and was way out of her league. But he didn't look like a druggie.

Of course, she had lousy man skills and was body-language illiterate, so what did she know? What she couldn't afford, though, was to be mixed up with a guy who played fast and loose with the law. Never again.

Suddenly as irritated with herself for wanting to cry as much as she was with Caleb for putting himself on the off-limits list, she scowled.

"If you're interested in drugs, you need to look somewhere else," she said in a chilly tone, wrapping her arms around herself to ward off the disappointment. She wished she hadn't scared away the comfort of the cat.

Caleb didn't say a word. He just arched a brow and continued to study her with those intense eyes of his. After a few seconds, she wanted to scream at him to say something. Anything. Or better yet, to leave. She couldn't pout properly with him there, staring.

"I didn't say I was interested in drugs," he finally said, stepping closer, invading her thinking space yet again.

"You—"

"No," he interrupted. "I said I'd heard you were the lady to talk to about hotting up my sex life."

Pandora bit her lip, mentally replaying their discussion. Had she jumped to conclusions? Was she so awkward at this flirtation thing that she'd misinterpreted a gorgeous man hitting on her?

Caleb reached out, rubbing the pad of his thumb over her bottom lip. Pandora barely held back her whimper as her entire body melted into a puddle of goo.

"I hate to see you damage such a pretty mouth," he murmured.

Nope. No misinterpreting that move. She didn't need a dictionary to define his meaning. Nerves simmered low in her belly. She wanted nothing more than to reciprocate the move. But as she'd told Caleb, and despite her teasing with Kathy, she wasn't in the market for a relationship.

Then again, Caleb Black wasn't a relationship kind of guy.

He was, however, a hot, sexy, have-a-wild-time and give-thanks-afterward kind of guy.

She didn't know if it was the freedom she felt in accepting that her only goal in being with him was to enjoy the ride.

Or maybe it was the sphere of calcite she'd taken to carrying in her pocket, hoping it'd help with her self-esteem.

Whatever it was, it was giving her a sense of purpose, a sense of self-confidence, that she welcomed with open arms.

She was so ready to give herself the best Christmas present ever. A guilt-free pleasurefest that she'd enjoy in decadent delight for as long as it lasted.

As far as gifts went, it beat the hell out of a new pair of slippers.

So when he rubbed her lip a second time, Pandora forced herself to dive out of the safety zone. She took a deep breath, then touched, just barely, the tip of her tongue to his thumb.

His eyes narrowed like golden lasers, then he grinned. A slow, wicked curve of his lips that set off warning bells in Pandora's head.

She was playing with fire.

After one last brush of his thumb across her oversensitized lip, his fingers caressed a gentle trail over her cheek, along her jaw, then down her throat. It was like being touched by a cloud, his fingers were so soft, so barely there.

Pandora stopped herself from whimpering.

"Is that why you came in here?" she asked breathlessly as his fingers worked their magic along her throat. A slide up, then down, sending tingles through her body. "Because you wanted to ask about aphrodisiacs?"

"Yes," he said, stepping closer. So close she could feel the heat of his body wrapping around her like a warm blanket of lust. "And no."

"Which?"

"Both."

His hand curved behind her neck, fingers tangling in her hair as he pulled her closer. Her head rested in his huge palm as she stared up into his eyes. He looked amused, but his dilated pupils and the tension in his jaw told her he was just as turned on as she was.

At least, that's how she was reading him.

Nerves, huge and frantic, scrambled in her stomach. But she had to know. Finding out how he would respond to her was worth the risk of rejection.

Pandora took that last step, closing the distance between them. Pretending her fingers weren't trembling, she pressed her hands against the cool leather covering Caleb's biceps. Even through the thick fabric, she could feel his muscles bunch tight.

"I wish you weren't wearing this jacket," she said, her words so low even she could barely hear them. But he heard. He gave her a long look that made her nipples harden, shrugged off the leather and tossed it on the counter.

Paulie instantly padded over and curled himself into a puddle on the discarded jacket, his black fur blending perfectly with the leather. Caleb grinned before turning his gaze back to Pandora. "Anything else?"

The mouthwatering sight of his arms, the muscles round and hard beneath the long sleeves of his T-shirt, made her want to wish he'd take that off, too.

But it was his amused reaction to her pet that sent her over the edge.

"I want a kiss," she told him. "A real one."

"I only do real," he countered, curving his hands over her hips and pulling her close. Close enough to feel that his arms weren't the only impressive muscles Caleb was sporting.

She wanted him to keep going. To take control, to kiss her crazy. But he didn't. It was as though he'd looked deep into her soul and saw how scared she was of taking center stage and being in charge, and was forcing her to face that fear if she wanted a taste of him.

Her head was spinning so fast, she needed to steady herself, and desperately wanted something to hold on to. Pandora gripped those deliciously hard arms and let her body melt into his.

She stood on tiptoe, her thighs brushing that hard length of his. Her nipples pebbled against his chest as she breathed in his scent. Excitement and anticipation fought for control of her emotions and she sucked in a breath. Then she did it.

She kissed Caleb.

And when her lips pressed against the firm fullness of his, it was suddenly the easiest hard thing she'd ever done in her life.

She wanted to close her eyes and sink into the pleasure. To hide, deep in the intense delight of his mouth on hers. But his gaze held hers captive.

Needing more, she gave in to the desire and slipped her tongue out to trace his lips. As if that's all he'd been waiting for, he suddenly turned voracious. His mouth took control. His tongue swept over hers, dancing at a wild pace that made her whimper and give over fully to the power of his kiss.

His fingers shifted from her hips to press, palms flat, against her butt. She almost purred with pleasure when she felt his rigid length—and holy cow, was he long!—pressing hard against her stomach.

Just as quickly as he'd gone wild, Caleb shifted into low gear. The wild, untamed intensity left his kiss and cool control took its place.

His mouth softened, his lips brushing gently over hers. His fingers unclenched, smoothing their way up to the small of her back as he pulled away, not completely, but enough that she couldn't revel in the power of his erection anymore.

Then, another brush of his lips, and he stepped away.

Oh, God. He was incredible. Eyes fluttering open, her knees wobbled as she settled her feet flat on the floor again.

Not caring if he saw how overwhelmed she was, Pandora closed her eyes and heaved a deep sigh. Then, meeting his gaze again, she bit her lip before forcing herself to step up to the plate.

All she wanted to do was strip that soft T-shirt off him so she could plaster herself against his hard chest before licking her way down his belly. His taste filled her senses, his scent wrapped around her and her butt still tingled from the pressure of his fingers.

He was like her every sexual fantasy come true.

But she'd been in trouble once already, with a guy who didn't even make the fantasy list. So she'd be an idiot not to make sure Caleb wasn't more trouble than she was willing to answer for.

"Can I ask you something?" she said softly. Needing every intuitive, people-reading skill she'd ever learned, and any that might be floating through her genes, she forced herself to relax and open her third eye. She scrunched her forehead, not feeling anything special there and settled for just relaxing. "And will you promise me you'll be honest?"

Her eyes locked with Caleb's. His gaze was intense, as if he was trying to read her mind before he committed. His shoulders were back, in honesty? Or braced for a hit?

She waited for him to tell her that she didn't have the right to ask for such a promise. She knew she didn't. Just because they were having a mind-blowingly sexual affair in her imagination didn't mean that in reality he owed her a damn thing.

But she couldn't risk her heart, her reputation or her fragile self-esteem on a man who broke the law. And even though she didn't trust her intuitive skills enough to believe she'd know if he lied, she needed to ask the question anyhow.

Finally, just as she was about to start fidgeting again, he nodded. Then he qualified his nod with, "You can ask whatever you want."

Good enough.

"Do you, um, are you into…" She bit her lip, wishing her cheeks weren't burning, then blurted out, "Do you do drugs?"

CALEB HAD BEEN ASKED that question plenty of times. And he'd always answered yes. More often, he didn't even have to answer, his image spoke for itself.

But this time…? He stared at Pandora, her hazel eyes wide but wary. He could still taste her, sweet and tempting. He was here in Black Oak for a reason. He had a crime to solve. And he'd never, ever, broken cover before. Not for anything, and especially not for a woman.

But with those pretty eyes staring at him, he saw only one option available.

Tell the truth.

"No," he answered. "I'm clean."

He watched her face, waiting to see the doubt. He told himself it didn't matter if she didn't believe him. After all, he'd spent six years crafting his image as a badass with drug connections. An image that had held up to South American drug lords, to the FBI and to L.A. street-gang leaders. An image that was based on the reputation he'd had growing up here in Black Oak.

Her sigh was so deep, the tips of her breasts singed his chest. Talk about a sweet reward for copping to the truth.

A part of him wanted to pull her close, just to wrap his arms around her and revel in the closeness. There was a sense of peace in Pandora, like a calm lake of serenity, that he craved desperately. At the same time, she made him want to strip her naked and lick her body from head to toe, seeing how many times he could make her come before he got to her feet.

Baffled by the conflicting emotions, both in direct opposition to his training and his own reticent nature, Caleb took a step back. He immediately missed the warmth of her body, the heat of her breasts against him. But he needed room to think. And to make sure he didn't screw up. His life might not be on the line this time, but his father's reputation was.

For what that was worth.

Caleb's mind raced, wondering whether he'd just made a major mistake. Time to do damage control.

"Not that I believe in aphrodisiacs, either," he told Pandora, needing to get them back on track.

And he might as well keep up this honest trend and see where it went. It was like following an unfamiliar road. There might be a treasure at the end. A very delicious, very sexy treasure. More likely, though, he'd slide right off some damn cliff.

She just laughed, though.

"Believing in aphrodisiacs is like believing in evolution. Some buy into the idea, some don't."

"Sure, but the theory of evolution has been around for,

well, ever. Sex food, though? Isn't that a by-product of the seventies?"

Amusement flared in her eyes as Pandora gave a shake of her head that indicated that he was a sad, misinformed man.

"Their history can be traced back centuries," she pointed out. "My great-great-great-grandmother was a wisewoman who created aphrodisiacs for royalty. Those were the kind of people who beheaded fakers, you know."

Caleb remembered Pandora's mother. Flowing dresses, fuzzy headpieces and huge jewelry glinting through mounds of long red hair. Her granny was a little fuzzier. He wasn't sure what the woman had looked like. His only impression was granola.

But Pandora looked... Well, normal. Not that that was saying much coming from a guy who spent most of his life around women who thought a G-string was ample coverage. Her hair fell in a smooth curtain, warm and sedate. She wore makeup, but nothing like the showgirl look he remembered her mother sporting. She wore a crystal on a chain around her neck, but her jeans and thick purple sweater seemed ordinary enough.

He looked around the café, noting the display of candles, pretty statues and chunks of rocks on the bistro tables. Circling the perimeter were bookcases, decks of cards and yes, a few crystal orbs and glittering things. He didn't know what most of the stuff was, but it didn't look that weird to him.

It looked pretty. Inviting, interesting and unthreatening. Word on the street, and his own impressions, said that was Pandora's doing. From what he'd heard, the store had been sinking to its death before she'd come along. Which just proved that she was a smart businesswoman. Not that she was weird.

And yet, she believed in aphrodisiacs? Really?

"This is all an act, though, isn't it?" he asked with a tilt of his head to indicate the most obvious New Agey thing he saw, a statue of a half-naked woman riding on the back of a flying dragon. "You're not telling me you really buy into all that…" Crap? "…stuff? Psychics and aphrodisiacs and woo-woo? Isn't it just a part of the show? Something to help sell a few candles and rocks?"

"Woo-woo?" she echoed, sounding as if the magical effects of his kiss had pretty well worn off. "Did you know the art of divination dates back to Greeks and Romans? Tarot cards to the Renaissance? Cleopatra used aphrodisiacs. This isn't a New Agey sales scam to buy into or not. And while these methodologies might have cultural stigmas, it's wrong to dismiss them as being part of a show."

Caleb mentally grimaced. He was usually better at gauging his quarry before he opened his mouth. But Pandora had a way of short-circuiting his brain.

"I'm not saying it's all bullshit. But you have to admit there're a lot of scams associated with this type of thing. And you don't come across as naive," he prevaricated. "I mean, your granny danced naked around the old oak at the base of the mountain, and your mom… Didn't your mom tell the future for dogs and cats?"

Her lips twitched, but she didn't let him off the hook. "My grandmother only danced naked on the full moon, and that was for religious reasons. And as for my mom… What? You don't think cats and dogs have futures?"

"Do you?"

"I do." She nodded, her hazel eyes wide and sincere. Caleb sighed, disappointment pouring through him as he revised his seduction plan. Then Pandora grinned. "But I doubt their thoughts and feelings can be scryed in their water dishes."

So used to being tense, he barely noticed himself relaxing under her smile. He did pay attention to the stirring interest his body felt, though, when he shifted a little closer so he could smell her sweet perfume again. It was a warm scent, making him think of a dark, mystical forest.

"So? What's the real deal? Are you a believer? Or are you just here to make a living?"

She narrowed her eyes, obviously sorting through his words. He liked watching her think. He'd just bet she had mental lists and a brain like one of those supercharged computers that'd calculate, analyze and summarize in seconds flat.

He gave in to temptation and reached out to rub a lock of her rich, thick hair between his fingers. It was as silky as it looked. He'd bet it'd feel even better sliding over his thighs.

"There's bullshit out there, sure," she acknowledged with the tiniest of nods. "There's a group, the Psychic Scenery tour bus, that stops here twice a year. These people travel all over the West Coast, visiting metaphysical stores and psychics, readers and healers. You could say they are the experts on the subject. Believe me, they've seen it all. And they never visit anyone or anywhere more than once if they deem it bullshit."

"How many times have they visited Moonspun Dreams?" he asked, both amused and impressed at how strongly she defended her store and her beliefs.

"Every spring and autumn for the last ten years," she said with just a hint of triumph in her smile. "Our store is one of the highlights of their tour, a selling point they use in their brochure."

"Because of the aphrodisiacs?" Tension he'd thought was gone returned to poke steely fingers in Caleb's back at the idea of hordes of people swarming into town looking for a sex fix. It was the perfect cover for moving drugs, and it pissed him off that Pandora was ruining his comfortable assurance that she was innocent.

"Oh, no," she told him. "I just opened the café two months ago, after the last tour. But I'm sure the regulars at Psychic

Scenery are going to be over-the-moon excited when they visit in April."

"Okay, so you're popular with these people and they're going to go crazy over your cookies when they visit. What does that have to do with whether or not you believe in all this?" he prodded.

He had no idea why he cared so much. Maybe it was the result of growing up the son of a clever con man. It'd taught him that people could sell a whole lot of things with a big fat smile on their face, even as they handed over a shopping bag filled with nothing but hot air.

That wasn't criminal. Not like selling drugs. But it'd sure as hell ruin the sweet image he had of Pandora to find out she was happily invested in selling lies.

"What that does is prove that we're time tested and cynic approved," she said. "I think there's a whole lot of stuff out there that we can't explain. I think some people tap into it more easily than others. And I think that believing has a power of its own."

"Isn't that the same thing as gullibility?" Caleb asked.

"Do you think that all this—" she waved her hand to indicate the store filled with the promise of magic "—is based on the power of suggestion?"

Caleb's brow shot up. She didn't sound offended. More like… Satisfied. Wasn't that interesting? Pandora was more intriguing by the second.

"Isn't most everything based on the power of suggestion?" he mused. "For instance, if I suggested that I'd like to kiss you again, you'd think about it, wouldn't you?"

Color washed from her cheeks, pouring down her slender throat and tinting the mouthwateringly showcased curves of her breasts with a pale pink glow. He wanted to touch and see if her skin was as warm as it looked.

"The brain is the most powerful erogenous zone," he told

her, his tone low. "Half of seduction takes place in the mind, first. Before I ever touch you, I could have you crazy with wanting me."

She bit her lip, her eyes huge as they darted from him to the store filled with customers just a few beads away.

Caleb gave her a smug wink as he leaned against a table, his feet crossed at the ankles and hands tucked in the front pockets of his jeans.

He was having fun. It'd been so long, he hadn't realized how good it could feel. At least for him. He wasn't so sure Pandora was the teasing type.

"And one meal of my aphrodisiacs could make you so turned on, you'd almost forget your own name," Pandora countered with a wicked smile at odds with the nerves dancing in her eyes. "You'd have the most delicious meal and the most memorable dessert you've ever dreamed of."

Even though his expression was as smooth as glass, Caleb was mentally reeling. What the hell? He blew out a breath, wanting to tug at the collar of his T-shirt. Yeah, she was pretty damn good at the teasing. Had she just propositioned him?

"What do you say?" Pandora prompted, her smile a soft curve of those luscious lips as she leaned against the counter so her hip bumped against his.

"You realize I'm attracted to you, regardless of what you serve for dinner," he said, trying to figure out what she thought a plate of oysters was going to do when he'd happily take her right then and there on the bistro table, in full view of her cats and anyone who walked by.

"Attraction is a necessary ingredient for an aphrodisiac to work," she explained quietly. "Unlike pharmaceuticals that change a person's will, aphrodisiacs are a natural enhancement. They make so-so sex fabulous. And great sex? Mind-blowing."

This time Caleb did run his finger around the collar of his shirt, needing to release a little of the heat. It was either that or grab her in front of her customers.

As if they knew he was about to pounce, a giggling pair of women walked through the beaded doorway. They both carried overflowing wicker shopping baskets. Looked as if Pandora was about to score.

In more ways than one.

"Fifi asked me to get more cookies," a guy said, sticking his shaggy head through the beaded curtain. "You have a few customers out here asking for them. You know the ones, the sexy cookies."

Pandora's gaze cut from him to Caleb, then back again. She looked torn, and just a little mischievous. He was afraid she'd drag the kid into this discussion to support her point.

"C'mon back, Russ," she said, her smile widening.

Time for him to get the hell out of there. Caleb grabbed his jacket, then leaned in close to whisper in Pandora's ear.

"Prove it to me."

6

This was the problem with wanting something as desperately as she wanted Caleb, Pandora mused. Once you got it, you had to figure out how the hell you were going to handle it.

"So what's the plan?" Kathy asked from her perch in a chair by the glistening lights of the three-foot-high Christmas tree with its shimmering golden balls and little red bows. "Are you ready for tonight?"

Ready? Biting her lip, Pandora scanned the plethora of food spread over the counter of the tiny cottage she was renting. Walking distance from the store, she'd chosen it for its location. Asparagus and oysters, celery and ginseng and chocolate. A roast was marinating in red wine and mushroom caps were waiting to be stuffed. All the fixings for an aphrodisiac-rich dinner for two.

Completing the theme, she'd brought home a dozen red candles for passion and had frankincense incense waiting to light.

"Maybe I shouldn't have him here," she worried. "I mean, it's like saying, 'Hey, eat up fast. I'm horny and wanna do it.'"

"Well, it's not like you could have him to dinner in the café. After all, you have a point to prove. And since it's one of those naked kind of points, it's better done in private, don't you think?"

"Naked…" Pandora pressed her palm against her belly, trying to quiet the butterflies flinging themselves against the walls of her stomach as they attempted to escape. "What the hell was I thinking?"

"That Caleb Black would look mighty fine naked," Kathy said with a wicked grin. Then her smile faded and she gave Pandora a searching look. "Are you sure you want to do this? You don't have to go through with the evening if you don't feel comfortable, you know. You can call it off, or just call it quits after dinner."

A part of Pandora grabbed on to that exit option like a lifeline. It was one thing to challenge Caleb face-to-face, when she was in the throes of sexual overload. But the idea of following through, here and now, once she'd had plenty of time to worry? That was something else entirely.

"I don't want to call the evening off," she decided. "I want this. I really do."

Sorta. She wanted the fantasy of having mind-blowing sex with Caleb. The man was obviously a sexual god. He was gorgeous. He was mouthwateringly sexy. He had that bad-boy, done-it-all and gone-back-for-seconds vibe going on.

And her? The naughtiest thing on her sexual résumé was wearing a see-through Santa nightie with black stiletto do-me boots.

"If you want him, and he wants you, then you'd be crazy to let nerves stop you. I mean, how many chances does a girl have for incredible sex?" Kathy challenged.

"Easy for you to say. You've already done one of the Black brothers," Pandora retorted.

"Yes, I did," Kathy said with a wicked smile, running her hand through the smooth curve of her hair. "Which is why I feel qualified to say do it, do it, do it."

Pandora laughed. Living close to Kathy was her favorite benefit to being back in Black Oak. A girl needed her best friend when she was gathering up the nerve to get naked with a guy.

"Okay, let's just say the night is great," Pandora suggested, pacing over to the tree to rearrange the bows and balls on the crisp evergreen boughs. Can't have the two gold balls next to each other, after all. It might ruin the ambience. "Say the sex is incredible. The best in my life. Maybe even one of his top ten. Multiple-orgasm, headboard-banging, seeing-stars incredible. Say it's all that. What do I do then?"

After a long pause, Kathy got to her feet and headed for the tiny kitchen.

"What are you doing?" Pandora called after her.

"Getting a glass of ice water."

"Seriously!"

"Seriously?" Kathy filled a cup with water from the pitcher in the fridge and gulped it down. "Seriously, then you'll probably collapse in an exhausted, albeit very satisfied, heap."

"But…" Pandora dropped onto the overstuffed chair, picking at the deep blue fabric with her fingernails. "But what if it's so great I want more? How did you have the greatest sex of your life, then walk away?"

"It's all about expectations," Kathy said, setting her water aside and coming over to sit across from Pandora. She leaned forward, her pretty face serious. "You know going in that it's special, that it's just that once, and you ring every drop of pleasure from it possible. Like seeing Baryshnikov dance, or visiting Stonehenge or meeting Johnny Depp at Comic-Con last year. They were all amazing experiences, but you don't expect to do them repeatedly, right?"

"What are the chances that sex with Caleb Black will be

as good as Baryshnikov, Stonehenge and the amazing Johnny Depp all rolled into one experience?"

"I think the chances are pretty damn good."

Pandora sank her head into the chair's pillowed back and sighed. She thought so, too.

"Look, you deserve this. Every woman deserves this. One night of absolute pleasure, with no strings or worries or stress. Just wild and mindless sex, with no rules or expectations."

"You think?"

"Don't you?"

Pandora looked at the array of food covering the two short countertops. Her grandmother's recipe book was there, too. Filled with recipes that had, so far, increased Moonspun Dreams' coffers beyond her wildest dreams.

Despite her run-don't-walk departure from all things associated with Black Oak and her mother, Pandora had been raised to believe certain things. And many of those tenets she still subscribed to wholeheartedly. Karma and the golden rule. Respecting nature and conserving resources. Prayer and faith. And as she'd told Caleb, she believed in what she did. In what the store offered.

Sure, she'd launched this aphrodisiac sideline as a desperate attempt to dig the store out of a financial pit. But obviously the aphrodisiacs worked. She saw proof five days a week between the hours of eleven and two, after all. All they required was a spark.

And even she had to admit, she'd definitely inspired a few sparks in Caleb.

"The bottom line is, do you want to do this?" Kathy prodded. "Or don't you?"

A thousand arguments still running through her head, Pandora sighed. Yes, she wanted it. It being this night with Caleb. And more important, a chance to step out of the shadows and have a little excitement in her life. The kind she'd enjoy, not the kind that made her cringe.

Pandora bit her lip again, then squared her shoulders and headed for the kitchen to wash her hands.

"What are you doing?" Kathy asked.

"Getting dinner started." She shot her friend a look of combined terror and excitement. "Who am I to deny myself the absolute pleasure I deserve?"

THREE HOURS LATER and that statement had become Pandora's mantra.

"I deserve absolute pleasure," she muttered to herself as she pulled a floaty black dress knitted of the softest cashmere over her shoulders and slipped the tiny mother-of-pearl buttons closed from cleavage to knee. The fabric molded gently over her breasts, showing just a hint of her red lace bra, and ended a few inches shy of her ankles, where she'd chosen to go barefoot except for a glistening ruby toe ring and gold anklet.

Not quite a see-through Santa nightie, she mused as she stared at her reflection, but it'd do. She fluffed her hair around her shoulders, added a smidge more mascara and took a deep breath.

"I do. I deserve absolute pleasure." The reminder had turned into an affirmation about an hour ago, but like most law-of-attraction-type things, she knew it was basically useless without real belief behind the words.

So she'd fake it. A quick glance at the clock told her that Caleb was due in five minutes. Which meant that as appealing as hiding under the bed was, she'd better get the appetizers ready.

Pandora hurried from the room, checking to see that the fire was burning bright in the fireplace and that all the red candles—for passion—were lit around the room. The cottage smelled delicious. The subtle waft of incense, the appealing scent of smoky apple wood. And the food.

That was the only thing she had complete confidence in tonight. Her food rocked. The roast was done and resting, tender and juicy in a gravy of rosemary, celery seed and just a pinch of ginseng. There wasn't really any aphrodisiac ingredients in the fresh rolls, but Pandora had filled in the menu with things that played to the theory that the way to a man's heart was through his stomach. If the rolls could open that door, she figured the aphrodisiacs should reroute things southward.

"Absolute pleasure," she murmured as she checked the chocolate-espresso mousse with whipped caramel crème in the fridge, then the wine that was breathing on the counter. Figuring it'd make her look less anxious, and might just help her chill out, she poured herself a glass.

"Yep, all ready for that pleasure. Absolutely."

The doorbell rang.

Pandora started, slopping wine all over her hand.

Right that second, if the cottage had a back door, she would have taken absolute pleasure in sneaking out through it.

Deep breath and a quick rinse of her fingers under the tap, she then wiped nervously down her dress before almost tripping over her own bare feet on the way to the door.

Another deep breath and she pulled it open.

"Hi," Caleb said.

Hubba da hubbada, her brain stuttered. Holy hunks, the man was pure eye candy. The moon at his back, his face was thrown into shadows. His black hair slicked down so it flowed like silk over his collar, he wore slacks, boots and a dark dress shirt. He smelled incredible. Male but with a hint of musk.

His smile was just this side of wicked as he gave her an

appreciative look, those warm gold eyes tracing her curves, from collar to breast, down her waist and over her hips until he reached her naked toes.

One look from him and she was ready to strip the rest of herself bare and see how many kinds of pleasure they could offer each other. Whether it was because he looked sexy enough to slurp with a spoon, because she was wearing her do-me undies, or if it was the day spent creating a meal meant for seduction, all Pandora could think about was how long she'd have to wait for dessert.

"Pandora?" he prompted, his smile tipping into a grin as he leaned his shoulder against the door frame. "You gonna let me in?"

Doh. They couldn't do dessert until he was inside, could they?

"I'm sorry. It's just… Wow." She stepped aside for him to enter. "You look fabulous."

Realizing how that'd probably sounded, color warmed Pandora's cheeks. "Not that you didn't look great before," she said. She winced, then tried again. "I mean, I wouldn't have thought you'd have dress clothes tucked away in your motorcycle saddlebags."

"Always pays to be prepared," he said as he dried his feet on the mat before entering the cottage. She shut the door behind him, its click echoing the beat of her heart in her chest.

"Do you have to dress up often?" she asked, suddenly realizing that she had no idea what Caleb did for a living. Gossip had run wild since his return to town last week, speculating on everything from career criminal to mechanic to construction. One person had thought he might even be a lawyer.

"It's the holidays," he said absently, looking around. "I figured I'd get roped into some Christmas fluff or other."

He gave her a slow smile, making her tummy slide down to her toes. "But this is a much better option."

Heat poured through Pandora's body like molten lava, hungry and intense.

She had to say something before she wrapped herself around his body and begged him to let her lick him from head to toe.

"So what do you do for a living?" she blurted out.

His smile changed. It was a tiny change, one she doubted most people would notice. It got a little hard, like his eyes. "I'm in the middle of changing jobs right now," he said.

Trying to study his body language without being obvious, Pandora bit her lip. Other than the slightly scary look in his eyes, he seemed totally relaxed. Did that mean he was out of a job, or just looking for something else before he left? And did it matter? It wasn't as if she needed to see his résumé. This was a one-night, prove-the-aphrodisiacs-work and have-great-sex fling.

So change the subject.

"Are you going to the big party tomorrow night at your father's motorcycle shop?" she asked.

His smile fell away, his shoulders tensed up. His body language had gone from friendly to unfathomable in less than a heartbeat. Her fault. She knew there were issues with him and his father. So she should have known that bringing him up wouldn't be a great conversation starter.

Wasn't she the hostess with the mostest.

"No."

Awkward.

Crazy with curiosity but not wanting to ruin the evening by asking more uncomfortable questions, Pandora was grateful when the oven timer went off.

"Please, make yourself comfortable," she invited as she hurried toward the safety of the food.

"I thought you'd be staying at Cassiopeia's place," Caleb said as he followed her into the kitchen.

Payback? She gave him an arch look over her shoulder, trying not to grin. Gotta love a guy who knew how to get revenge without drawing blood.

"Oh, no," she said, laughing a little at the idea of staying in her mother's. It would be like staying on a movie set. Nobody who knew Cassiopeia ever had to ask if she believed in the woo-woo. She lived it, right down to the celestial designs on her carpet.

Pandora pulled the roasted asparagus from the oven and set it on the stove top, then turned back to Caleb.

"No. My mother's house is too crowded for me. She collects as much stuff there as she does in the store, plus there are always people in and out when she's home. Even now, with me just stopping by to collect her mail and water the plants, they pop in hoping for a reading or chat. I think it drives her nearest neighbor, the mayor, a little crazy."

Caleb flashed a quick grin as he handed her a bottle of wine. She glanced at the label and raised her brows. Pricey.

"I forgot my aunt had moved."

"Haven't you been to see her yet? I hear she throws a huge holiday open house. Is that next weekend? Someone was saying that your dad never goes, but you probably will, right?" Busy setting the mushroom caps and oysters Rockefeller on a serving plate, it took her a few seconds to pick up on the sudden tension in Caleb.

She'd done it again.

"I'm sorry. I don't mean to make you uncomfortable by bringing up your father." She met his eyes. He didn't look uncomfortable anymore, though. More like…intrigued.

"Don't worry about it. If I had a problem talking about Tobias, I'd say so."

"Okay," she said slowly. Except that he didn't talk about

his father. Or his family at all. Despite the tension and hurt she saw in his face, she had to know more. Was desperate to understand more about Caleb Black. So she quirked a brow and continued, "Although I haven't seen her since I moved back, or since she became mayor for that matter, I do remember your aunt. I'm not sure she's a fan of my mother's, though. Mom said the week after she moved in, Her Honor raised the fence height in her backyard and instructed the gardener to plant a hedge between the houses."

Caleb snickered.

"Aunt Cynthia is a hard-ass all right," he agreed. "It must drive her insane having a free spirit like your mom next door. Probably afraid people will think she and Cassiopeia are having wild parties in the hot tub after dark."

Pandora laughed, her nerves over the evening starting to fade as he pulled out a chair and got comfortable. She held up the bottle of wine in question, and when he nodded, got him a glass from the counter.

"I guess you've worked really hard to distance yourself from your dad," she said as she poured.

"It wasn't hard. I just had to move out of Black Oak and his sphere of influence."

"Smart," she complimented. Then, honesty forced her to admit, "Tobias comes into the store and the café pretty regularly. Having a parent with an, um, forceful personality myself, I can understand how it'd be challenging to live with such a strong person. But I have to admit, I do like him."

She didn't add the bit of gossip she'd heard earlier that day, that Tobias had hooked up with that nasty piece of work, Lilah Gomez. Telling a man his dad was dating someone younger than him was hardly dinnertime conversation.

"Most people like Tobias," Caleb said with a shrug. "He's got a way with the charm."

"Like father like son?" She smiled, handing him the glass of wine.

"You're kidding, right?" Caleb shook his head, obviously not seeing himself as a charmer. "I was a disappointment on that score. Maya's got a way about her, that's for sure. But Gabriel got the bulk of the charm. Me, I got the short end of that particular stick."

Pandora wanted to tell him just how appealing rough edges could be, but took a sip of her wine instead. Then she gathered her nerve and lifted the platter filled with the promise of sexual nirvana.

"Speaking of sticks and their length," she said with her naughtiest smile, "I have your proof here. If you'd care to give it a try?"

Caleb swore he felt the energy in the room shift. Friendly good humor changed to a sexual thrum in the blink of Pandora's hazel eyes.

Not that he minded, but there had been something nice in that friendliness. He didn't think he'd ever been friends with a woman. Coworker, acquaintance, lover. That was about it.

But, hey. He'd be an idiot to complain about stepping over to the sexy side. And a bigger idiot to regret having her take away something he hadn't even realized he might want to enjoy a little longer.

"Proof, huh?" he challenged as he took an appetizer from the tray and inspected it. "Looks like any other stuffed mushroom. How's this proof?"

"Mushrooms and sausage together are a strong aphrodisiac," she assured him before she bit into one herself.

Caleb had his doubts, but he had just enough of his father's fabled charm to know better than to call his hostess a liar. Especially when she looked so sexy sitting across from him.

So he took a mushroom.

By the end of the meal, Caleb realized two things.

One, he'd never spent this long with a hard-on, and not done anything about it, in his life.

And two, he'd never talked—just talked—to a woman before like this. By unspoken agreement, they'd avoided the biggies like family and career. Instead, they'd shared their favorite Christmas memories, discovered they had the same taste in music and movies, and debated the merits of paperbacks versus ebooks.

It was like an actual date. Caleb had always wondered if that getting-to-know-a-person-on-a-date thing was real or just a myth. But this was, other than the painful pressure against the zipper of his slacks, totally awesome.

"Dessert?" she offered, noting he'd cleaned his plate for the third time. She'd been a little more delicate in her eating, only having one helping.

Despite his gluttony, Caleb glanced at the rich, chocolaty mounds of fluff with the caramel topping and sprinkling of nuts and his mouth watered.

"Sure," he agreed. Then he realized he'd better clear some stuff up before they got into anything else that made his mouth water.

"But here's the thing," he said once she'd served them both and sat back down at the table. Then she started fiddling with the button, just there at the very center of her cleavage, and he forgot what he'd wanted to say.

Instead, he focused on the silky smoothness of her pale skin. Unlike most redheads, she was freckle free. At least, she was as far as he could see. Instead, her skin was almost translucent. Delicate.

"Caleb?" she said.

He dragged his eyes away from the contrast of the rich black fabric against the tempting swell of her breasts.

"Huh?" he asked, meeting her amused gaze. His lips quirked, knowing he deserved that look.

"The thing?" she prompted.

"The thing…" He frowned, thinking back. "Yeah, here's the thing. This meal was delicious."

Her smile was slow and sweet, those full lips curving in delight as she reached across the tiny table and rubbed her hand over his. Caleb's dick reacted as if she'd licked it.

"Thanks," she said softly. "I'm so glad you enjoyed it."

"I did. And I'm sure I'm going to enjoy this dessert just as much," he assured her, gesturing with the spoon he'd picked up. "But as great as it all was, I'm not getting how you think this proves that aphrodisiacs work."

Pandora gave a slow nod, as if she was agreeing, or at least considering his words. Then instead of picking up her spoon, she swiped her finger through the caramel-drizzled whipped cream.

Caleb tensed.

She lifted her cream-covered finger to her mouth, then rubbed it over her lip, licking the sweet confection away with a slow swipe of her tongue.

Caleb's eyes narrowed. He tried to swallow, but his throat wasn't working right.

Some cream still on her finger, Pandora sucked it into her mouth, her lips closing around the tip just enough so he could still see the pink swirl of her tongue as she licked it away.

Son of a bitch.

He swore he could smell the smoke as his brain short-circuited.

When she reached back into that crystal bowl and scooped up more dessert, this time cream and chocolate both, Caleb held his breath.

But instead of repeating the tasting show, she leaned forward to reach across the table. The move made her dress, unbuttoned so temptingly, shift to show more of the red lacy fabric of her bra. Before he could groan at the sight, though, she offered that fingerful of temptation to him.

"Taste?" she said, her words low and husky.

As hard as it was not to stare at the bounty bound in red lace, his gaze locked on hers. Her eyes were slumberous. Still sweet, he didn't think anything could change that. But sexier. There was a knowledge in them that said she knew exactly what she was doing to him. And that she planned to do a hell of a lot more.

Holding her gaze, he wrapped his fingers around her wrist, bringing her hand to his mouth. The chocolate was rich, with a hint of coffee. Her finger tasted even better. He sucked the sweet confection off her flesh, then ran his tongue along the length of her palm, scraping his teeth against the mound at the base of her thumb.

Pandora gave a little mewl of pleasure.

Caleb grinned.

"So…" she said after clearing her throat.

"So?"

"So that's the thing."

Caleb frowned.

"You said you wanted me. And I obviously am attracted to you," she told him, gently extricating her fingers from his hand.

"Yeah?"

"But let's face it. I'm not your type. I'm what's usually termed a good girl."

"How good are you?"

"Really, *really* good," she promised. "But you don't do good girls. You're a quick and painless, love 'em and leave 'em kind of guy. You keep life, and sex, commitment-free and just a little distant."

Caleb frowned, not sure he liked how well she read him.

"So?"

"So that's my proof," she said.

Before he could point out that it really wasn't proof, she held out her hand. He took it, getting to his feet. She didn't move back, though. So his body brushed against her smaller, more delicate figure.

"Your proof is that we're not each other's type?"

"That," she agreed, turning to lead the way out of the kitchen. Then she looked over her shoulder and said, "And the fact that you're not the kind of guy to sleep with a good girl."

He couldn't deny that truth. In the two days since she'd challenged him and tonight, he'd made some inroads, buddying up with one of the drug dealers unhappy with his slow move up the food chain. He'd come to dinner with the idea of finding out more about her little aphrodisiac sideline. He'd planned to subtly grill her about what she might have seen in the alley between her building and Tobias's.

Despite the excuse for their date, he'd had no intention, none at all, of getting naked with her. But he still wasn't giving credence to some crazy food combination. Nope, the credit for that was all Pandora's.

Before he could tell her that, she stopped in the middle of the living room and turned to face him. She was so close, he could see the beat of her heart against her throat.

He could see the nerves in her eyes, there just beneath the desire. The nerves didn't bother him, though. They were a lot more exciting than acceptance or complacency.

"We spent the last hour and a half talking," she told him. "There was no flirting. No innuendo or teasing or sexual promises, right?"

Caleb frowned as the truth of her words hit him. He'd spent the entire meal horny as hell. Hornier than he'd been with any other woman in his life.

But again, that was due to Pandora. Not the food.

"What's your point?"

And then those delicate fingers skipped down the row of pearly buttons, unfastening her dress as they went. Caleb had faced strung-out drug dealers shoving guns in his gut and kept his cool. But the minute that dress cleared her belly button, he swore the room did a slow spin.

Damn, she was incredible.

She walked toward him, the black dress hanging loose from her shoulders to her belly.

When she reached him, Caleb's hand automatically gripped her hips. She smiled, then leaned even closer so her body pressed tight against his. She reached between them and slid her palm over the hard length of his erection, making his dick jump desperately against the constraining fabric of his slacks.

He groaned in delight.

"And that's the proof that the aphrodisiacs work," Pandora told him just before she pressed her mouth to his.

7

WHEN NERVES MADE HER WANT to turn around and run, Pandora reminded herself that the best things in life were worth fighting for. Even if that meant fighting her own fears.

When her fingers trembled, she just dug them tighter into the deliciously muscled expanse of Caleb's shoulders. He felt so good. Strong and solid and real.

She wasn't going to chicken out, dammit. This was her one and only opportunity for awesome, aphrodisiac-inspired sexual bliss. The experience of a lifetime with a man reputed to be incredible.

So when her knees wobbled, she leaned forward, resting her hips against his for support.

Yeah, baby. There it was.

A whole lot of long, hard, throbbing nirvana.

He wanted her, just as much as she wanted him. Proof was right there, pressing insistently against her belly.

Hello, baby, her body sighed.

"More," she demanded against Caleb's lips.

He gave her the more she asked for, then even more than she'd dreamed. He made her feel like the only woman in his world.

Caleb's mouth slid over hers, taking the kiss from soft, wet heat to intense, raging passion with a slip of his tongue. His hands settled on the curve of her waist, pulling her tighter against that promising ridge pressing against his zipper.

Pandora melted.

She twined her arms around the back of his neck, holding tight as their tongues danced a wild tango. Anticipation coiled tighter in her belly when his fingers slipped up her side, from her waist to the curve of her breast. Her nipples ached with the need to feel his fingers, to know how he'd touch her.

Would he be gentle and sweet? Or wild and demanding?

Wanting desperately to know, she eased back. Not her mouth. Oh, no, she wasn't giving up one second of this delicious kiss. And her hips were fused, as if of their own volition, to his. Although she was pretty sure she could ease back a few inches and still feel the thick heat of his erection pressing in temptation against her stomach.

Instead, she eased her shoulders back. Just a little.

And purred in delight when he proved to be as clever as he was gorgeous, taking the invitation and curving his fingers over the heavy, aching weight of her breast. Her nipple beaded tighter against the erotically scratchy lace of her bra as he circled his hand in a slow, tempting spiral.

Had she ever been this turned on? Heat swirled through her body like a whirlwind. Building, twisting, teasing. Higher and higher, tighter and tighter.

He squeezed. She gasped, moaning and leaning into his hand.

"More," she demanded again.

His hand didn't leave her breast, but the other moved higher up her back. She felt a tiny snap as the hooks gave way. The straps of her bra sagged, slipping down her shoulders.

Before she could decide if this was good or bad, his fingers skimmed under the fabric and flicked her nipple. Like an electric shock, the sensation shot through her body with a zinging awareness. Pandora whimpered, shifting left, then right, as her favorite sexy panties dampened with evidence of her need.

"I like how you follow directions," she said against his lips, her laugh only a little bit nervous.

"Let's see how you do," he returned, leaning back so he could see the bounty he'd released. "Take it off."

"I beg your—"

"Off," he demanded. To emphasize his command, he took those amazing hands off her and stepped backward. Pandora wanted to whimper. She wasn't sure if it was over the loss of his magic fingers, the denial of his body. Or if it was pure embarrassment of having him this focused on her body. It wasn't bad, but it wasn't centerfold quality, either.

Blushing, Pandora twitched the sides of her dress inward. She didn't pull it closed. She didn't want to send a message that playtime was over. But, still, she wasn't sure she wanted to play peekaboo like this.

"C'mon, Pandora. I want to see." His words were husky. His vivid gold eyes were intense and just a little needy.

"Wouldn't you rather taste?" she asked with her most wicked sexy look.

"I'm the kind of guy who likes to cover all the bases," he said with a grin. He sounded relaxed, but she could see the heat in his eyes, the tightness of his body. The oh-my-God huge ridge pressing against his zipper. "So let's start with the visual, then we'll move on to the other senses."

She wanted this, she reminded herself. Wanted to be front and center of attention. And even more, she wanted Caleb. Wanted a night of mindless, wild sexual exploration.

Which meant she had to step up to the plate and play the game. With that reminder ricocheting around her head, Pandora lifted her chin, then took a step backward.

She released the edges of her dress, rounding her shoulders for just a second so her bra straps slipped down under the sleeves, catching on her upper arms. Caleb's eyes were like lasers, sharp and intense as he stared.

She skimmed her fingers up her bare abdomen and cupped her lace-covered breasts. His stare intensified. Pandora's fingers folded over the top of the cups of her bra in preparation for tugging it down. But she couldn't do it.

It was as if her shyness was in battle with the power of Caleb's sexual magnetism, amplified by the aphrodisiacs. She wanted this, like crazy. But it scared her.

Slowly, her eyes still locked on his, she turned. Back to him, her head angled so she could still see him, she pulled the bra straps off her arms, under the fabric of her dress, then let the bra dangle at her side.

"Toss it aside," he ordered.

She tossed it toward the couch, the red lace catching the edge of one magenta pillow and hanging there like a flag of surrender.

"Turn around," he commanded. His voice was husky, his body tense. He looked like the bad boy that rumor claimed him to be. He didn't scare her, though. Instead, his demeanor made her feel…amazing. Sexy and strong.

All because he looked at her as if she was the hottest thing he'd ever seen. The answer to all his sexual fantasies, even.

Holding on to that thought, Pandora turned.

As she faced him again, Caleb kept his eyes on hers for three beats, then dropped his gaze. He arched a brow at her hands clutching the filmy fabric of her dress closed, so she let it go and dropped her arms to her sides. As her breath shuddered in and out, the fabric shifted, sliding over her rigid nipples, adding a whole new layer to the torturous delight going through her body.

He stepped closer. He reached up, his fingers tracing her

areola, visible through the veil of black fabric. Her nipples beaded tighter. Heat circled low in her belly, making Pandora press her thighs together to intensify the wet delight.

His gaze shifted, meeting hers.

His eyes were molten gold. Slumberous and sexy.

"Nice," was all he said, though.

Before she could ask him what that was supposed to mean, he leaned forward and took the opposite nipple into his mouth, sucking on it through the fabric. The wet heat of his lips, combined with the subtle abrasion of the material, made her gasp in delight.

Desire melted her body. Her knees felt soggy, so she grabbed on to him to keep her balance.

"You like?" he asked, his teeth scraping over the aching tip before he sucked again.

"I really, really like," she hoarsely agreed.

Her fingers scraped a gentle trail over the wide breadth of his shoulders, then down until she reached those freaking rock-hard biceps. She gave a low growl deep in her throat as she tried to wrap her hands around his arms. Too big, too large, too wide. She hoped that meant other things were big and wide, too.

He swept his hand up the opening of the fabric, his palm hard and warm as it skimmed her body, leaving a trail of tingling awareness behind. He cupped her breast, his long fingers squeezing in rhythm as he sucked.

Her body went into heavenly spasms. Wet heat pooled between her legs, emphasizing the aching pressure building there. So needy she wanted to beg, Pandora wrapped one calf around his leg, pressing tight to try to relieve the ache.

He growled his approval. Then he grabbed her butt with both hands and lifted, making Pandora squeak in shock. Not lifting his mouth from her breast, he swung her around so her back was against the wall, anchored between it and the hardness of his body.

"Oh, yeah," she murmured, letting her head fall back with a thud. It was definitely easier to focus on the pleasure if she didn't have to worry about not falling on her ass.

Finished playing through the fabric, Caleb pushed open her dress and gave a low, husky growl at the sight of her bare breasts. Pandora knew her chest was flushed almost as pink as her nipples, but she didn't care. She loved his reaction. Loved the appreciative heat in his eyes and the way his fingers tightened on her waist as he stared.

"Kiss me," she whispered.

Caleb's eyes met hers and she swallowed the sudden lump in her throat. His gaze was hungry, but there was an appreciation, a sort of soft wonder, in his eyes that made her feel as if she was the most incredible woman in the world.

Then his mouth met hers and she forgot to think at all. His tongue caressed, then slipped gently between her lips. He tasted delicious. Hot and mysterious, with just a hint of chocolate. As he kissed her, his hands slid up to gently cup her cheeks, tilting her head to the side just a little so his mouth could better access hers.

Pandora swore she was melting. Not just sexually, although one more rub of his thigh against hers and she'd explode. But emotionally. The kiss was pure romance. Sweetly sensual, sexually charged and oh, so perfect.

Then he changed the angle. His mouth devoured. His hands skimmed over her shoulders, taking her dress down her arms. He gripped her hips for just a second, pulling her body away from the wall so the fabric could fall free to the floor.

Leaving her naked, except for her tiny little black panties.

She shivered as his fingers, just the tips, trailed a path along her spine. Up to her shoulder blades, where with the gentlest of pressure, he pressed her bare breasts tighter against his chest. Down to the small of her back, right above her butt, where his fingers curved down beneath the strip of elastic and gripped her buns. His fingers grazed her thigh, leaving heated trails of pleasure.

The move brought Pandora closer, so she locked her calf around the back of his knee and hugged tight, trying to relieve some of the pressure building between her thighs, swirling and tightening. Her breath came in gasps now as his fingers slipped around her hip, tracing the elastic of her panties. First at her belly, then around her thigh.

She shifted her knee, pulling back just a little. Inviting his fingers. Hoping he'd take the hint and touch her. She needed him to touch her, to drive her those last crazy steps over the edge.

But he just kept tracing the elastic. Caressing in soft, teasing moves.

He wasn't trying to drive her to passion, he was just driving her insane.

"More, dammit," she said against his mouth.

Then she felt his kiss shift as he grinned. Before she could decide if she was amused or irritated that he'd made her beg, his fingers slipped beneath the silk of her panties and found her.

They traced her swollen folds, teasing, stroking, enticing. Pandora swirled her hips, matching her rhythm to the dance of his fingers.

His mouth left hers to trail kisses, tiny sweet kisses, over her jaw and down the smooth flesh of her throat, laid bare as she tilted her head back against the wall.

His head dipped lower.

Her heart pounded harder.

His fingers slipped, first one, then two, then three, into the hot slick heat of her welcoming flesh.

Her breath came in pants.

His fingers thrust. In, then out. In, then out.

His lips closed over the rigid, pouting tip of her breast, sipping and laving the aching bud in time with his dancing fingers.

Pandora's head spun. Heat coiled, tight and low. Her hips twisted, shifted, undulating in time with the thrust of his fingers. Need screamed through her, demanding release.

Then he flicked his thumb over her slick folds.

And she exploded.

She cried out in delight as the climax pounded through her, taking her over once, then twice. Her body rang with pleasure. The lights of the Christmas tree flashed before her eyes, echoing the fireworks exploding in her mind.

It wasn't until she floated back to earth a couple of minutes—or years—later, that she realized he'd wrapped his arms around her in a soothing, rocking sort of hug.

Pandora's heart dissolved into a gooey mess.

"See," she murmured against the hard comfort of his shoulder, curving in tighter as he hugged her close. "Told you it'd be great."

"Great?"

"Incredible? Amazing? Mind-blowingly awesome?" she returned, leaning back to smile up at him.

He returned her smile, brushing a damp tendril of hair off her face with gentle fingers.

"Sweetheart, don't get me wrong. This was, and will continue to be, incredible. But in the spirit of honesty, I need to tell you something."

Oh, God. Tell her what? Was she doing it wrong? Passion fleeing Pandora's head like fog in the morning sun, she pulled back to stare in horror. "What?"

Other than his arched brow, his gorgeous face was unreadable.

"You're hot," he assured her. "And this intensity, the chemistry between us, is amazing."

Horror was replaced by confusion. "So…what's wrong?"

"Wrong? Babe, this is way too good to be wrong. No, nothing's wrong. I'm just saying that you had a point here and I don't think you're going to prove it."

"A point?" She'd had a point? Something beyond an orgasm or three?

"You said you were gonna prove that your aphrodisiacs work, remember?" he said with a grin. "I'm still wondering what you're gonna offer up as proof."

Oh. That.

Relief washed over her in a wave, making her want to drop to the couch and sigh in thanks.

"Proof?" she said, her words husky against the soft dusting of hair on his chest. "The proof will be you panting, exploding with an orgasm."

He groaned, his fingers combing through her hair. She could feel his laughter, though, as his chest vibrated against her mouth.

Her lips still exploring his chest, Pandora forced her eyes open to give him an arch look of inquiry.

"Sweetheart, you're hot. I'm wild for you. So the orgasm, that's a given."

She liked that. Wild for her. Pandora shivered in delight, thrilled beyond delight that a guy like Caleb wanted her this much.

"It *is* a given," she agreed. "It definitely is. But you'll be coming before you get your boots off."

His laughter wasn't so silent now.

"That hasn't happened since I was fifteen."

"Kiss that memory goodbye, then," she instructed. "Because thanks to me, and my aphrodisiacs, you'll never be able to say that again."

She didn't know where the words came from. But once they were out, she wasn't scared. Instead, she was empowered. Inspired. Excited.

It was like someone had just broken her from a prison she hadn't realized she'd spent her life in.

And now she was free. Free to enjoy, free to explore. And most of all, free to use Caleb's body for every single kinky sexual fantasy she'd ever had.

CALEB LAUGHED AS PANDORA twirled one finger in the air to indicate they should switch places. She thought she was going to take control of the fun. Not likely. He never, ever gave up control.

But neither did he deny a lady her pleasure.

So in the name of humoring her, he released her leg to let the silky-smooth length of it slide down his thigh. Then, his hands wrapped around her waist, he lifted her and twirled, so they'd changed positions.

"Now what?" he challenged, grinning.

She looked so earnest.

Her hair was a silky cloud around her face, rumpled and glowing in the light of the fire. Hazel eyes, still hazy with pleasure, studied him as though she was figuring out a puzzle. Good luck with that, he thought.

"It's time," she intoned with a smile.

"Go for it," he invited, trying not to laugh.

It wasn't that he didn't think she was gorgeous. Sweet and pretty and so damn sexy. She was all that. But she was hardly a practiced seductress. So he figured this was going to be a hot and sexy time, but he wasn't too worried about control.

Or the state of his boots.

"See, here's the thing, though," she said slowly, her words as soft as the fingers she was tracing down his chest.

"Which thing is that?"

She gave him a chiding look, then shrugged a little, making her breasts bounce and his mouth water.

"The thing is, I'm new to seduction."

Caleb laughed, then grabbed her hands and lifted them to his lips, pressing kisses on her knuckles. "Sweetie, you don't have to do anything you don't want to."

"Oh, but there is so much I do want to do. I'm just letting you know, ahead of time, in case I drive you too crazy, too fast," she said, her smile turning wicked.

His laughter turned a little hoarse as she pulled her hands away and planted them directly on his belt buckle. Talk about getting right to business. Not that he objected, but he'd been kinda looking forward to a little bit of what he'd imagined would be shyly sweet exploration.

She didn't tug his buckle open, though. Instead, she slipped her fingers inside his jeans and caught hold of his shirt, pulling it free. Her palms flat against his belly, she slid them upward, taking his shirt with them. Following her cue, he lifted his arms, then finished it off himself, tossing it toward the same couch currently holding her bra.

One for one, they were on a roll.

"Mmm," she hummed, staring at his chest as if she was mesmerized. Caleb was already sporting a pretty nice erection, but that look on her face, pure appreciative awareness, made his dick throb.

Her palms still flat, she smoothed them over his shoulders, her fingers warm and teasing as they skimmed his skin. Her nails scraped a hot trail of fire down his arms, pausing to curve over biceps that, yes, he knew it was stupid, but he flexed a little. Her soft sigh of appreciation didn't make him feel stupid, though. It made him feel like a freaking superhero.

Her eyes flicked to his, then back to his chest. But he saw a wicked light in their depths. Like she was up to something.

Not wanting to ruin her fun and tell her there wasn't anything he hadn't seen or done, he relaxed and waited.

Then she pressed her mouth, hot and wet, against his nipple. And he damn near exploded.

What the hell? Her hands were skimming, caressing their way over his chest, but it was her mouth that was driving him crazy. Her tongue slipped out, tasting, testing. Tempting. Since she hadn't made a rule against it, Caleb grabbed on to the silky warmth of her waist before sliding one hand up to cup the weight of her breast. Fair was fair, after all.

Apparently she wasn't interested in fair, though.

Pandora shifted, trailing those hot, openmouthed kisses down his chest.

Caleb was going insane. That was the only justification he could find for his inability to hold on to any semblance of control.

For a man who prided himself in his skill, both with women, and over his body, he didn't know what to do here. How to react. It was as if Pandora had woven a magical spell over him. Like she was an addiction, one he couldn't resist.

Her lips, wet and silky, trailed lower down his belly, the rasp of his zipper filling the room as her teeth tugged it down.

Caleb groaned, his fingers clenched in her soft hair. He realized he didn't give a damn.

She could keep the power.

Just as long as she continued driving him crazy.

Then her lips pressed against the tip of his dick.

Caleb growled a combination of shock and pleasure. Taking that as a go-ahead, she tugged his shorts and pants down below his knees, then her fingers trailed a teasing path back up his thighs.

She pulled back, just a little, and looked up at him. With those deceptively innocent hazel eyes locked on his, she leaned forward and wrapped her lips around the throbbing head.

He almost yelped in surprise. Then he closed his eyes, enjoying the delight of her mouth.

She was so good at this. She licked and nibbled him like a freaking lollipop.

Intense pleasure pounded through him, demanding release. Her mouth felt like heaven, the kind that only bad boys got into. Her tongue swirled, then she sucked. Hard.

He damn near exploded.

"No," he shouted instead.

"No," he repeated, gentling it this time and soothing his hands over the tangle his fingers had made in her hair. "Not like this. The first time I come, I want it to be inside you."

Her brow arched and she leaned forward again, but he gripped her hair. "Not inside your mouth, either."

Her smile was a work of art. And not just because she offered it up from her knees in front of his bare, throbbing erection. He reached out and pulled her to her feet, needing to kiss her almost as much as he needed to come.

"More," he said, borrowing her earlier demand.

"Definitely more," she gasped, wrapping her arms around his neck and kissing him back. Before he could get too serious about it, though, she pulled away.

"Hey!"

"I don't think we want these in the way," she teased, shimmying out of her panties. She hurried over to her purse and grabbed something, showing off the condom with a grin before sauntering back.

Not trusting his body to behave if she touched him again, he held up one hand to indicate she stay where she was. Then he took the condom and slipped it on, reveling in the view as he protected them.

"You're beautiful," he told her, pulling her toward him. "I want you so much."

"How much, exactly?" she teased.

"This much."

Done talking, he grabbed her tight and took her mouth in a deep, devouring kiss. Her moan of delight was all he needed to know she was ready. He grasped her hips, his hands curving into her butt and lifting. Her arms tight around his shoulders, she wrapped her legs around his hips.

In one quick, delightful thrust, Caleb was inside her. She was tight, hot and wet. Delicious. His hands gripping her hips, he thrust, his hips setting a fast rhythm.

"More," she breathed against his throat as she undulated in a tempting dance, pulling him in deeper.

Deeper and deeper. Harder and faster.

Her moans became whimpers. Her breath heated his neck as she dug her fingernails into his shoulders, gripping him so tight her heels dug into the small of his back.

He couldn't think.

All he could do was feel the incredible sensations building. Tightening. Need pounded at him. Her mewling pants were driving him higher.

Then she came. Her gasp was followed by the soft chanting of his name. Over and over and over, she called out to him.

He couldn't restrain himself any longer. As her body spasmed and contracted around him, he exploded in delight.

His mind spinning, aftershocks of the sexual blast still zinging through his body, Caleb let his head fall back against the wall. He unclenched his fingers from the soft cushion of Pandora's butt to let her slide her legs back to the floor. She puddled against him like a purring kitten, nuzzling her head under his chin and giving a moaning sort of sigh that made him feel like king of the sex gods.

"Bed?" he groaned against the warm, smoothness of her throat.

"That door over there," she murmured, her words more a husky purr than anything. Caleb forced his eyes open, looking around for *over there*. There were two doors, one cracked open enough that he could see was a bathroom. Handy. The other was closed. There was a bed waiting on the other side of that door.

The trick was to get to it.

He had a whole lot of warm, wonderful woman wrapped in his arms.

His slacks were around his ankles. Pure class, he thought as he rolled his eyes. His boots were still laced tight, so he couldn't kick his pants off and romantically sweep Pandora into his arms.

Romantically. Holy crap. A hard-core realist, Caleb knew the effects drugs could have on the body. But asparagus and oysters? That all-natural aphrodisiac thing was pure bullshit.

At least, he'd thought it was until now, as he stood with his head still reeling, his jeans jammed down around his socks like a pimply faced adolescent getting it for the first time behind the school gym.

Now? Now he was thinking up ways to be romantic.

Again…holy crap.

Pandora gave a sighing little wiggle, her curves pressing tighter against him, the deliciously pebbled hardness of her nipples scraping against his chest and her flowery-scented hair rubbing under his chin.

A part of him—he swore it was Hunter's voice—was kicking in to lecture mode. He shouldn't be doing this. The plan was to use her store's proximity to keep an eye on his father. Not to use her, in any way, shape or form.

But was it using? his body argued. He was seriously interested in her. She was gorgeous and sexy and fun. And this didn't have to get in the way of his investigation, so what did it matter?

Who gave a damn how he'd got here.

Caleb vowed in that second, as he brushed a soft kiss against the top of her head, that he was going to enjoy the hell out of this night. Whatever was driving it, he was the one having the fabulous ride.

Well, he and Pandora.

And it was time to make sure she got a ride she'd never forget, either.

"Round two," he promised. "This time, I'll show you what I can do with my boots off."

8

"WELL?" KATHY PRODDED in a frantic admonition, leaning across the sales counter so far her butt was almost up in the air. "I can't believe you didn't call me last night to tell me about your dinner. I'm your best friend. Your confidante. Your coconspirator of all things naughty. And I have to drag myself out of bed on a cold Saturday morning and brave the crazy shoppers to nag you into filling in the deets?"

A little freaked at the idea of verbalizing all the images that'd been playing in Technicolor through her head all day, Pandora rolled her eyes. She was trying her best to ignore Kathy's chipper curiosity. Especially since the store *was* filled with holiday shoppers, all with varying degrees of gossip expertise.

Trying to act professional, she struggled to wrap gold foil paper around an octagon-shaped box while the customer tapped her foot impatiently in time with "Jingle Bells" playing through the store's speakers.

"Whose idea was it to offer free gift wrapping?" she muttered as the tape stuck to the wrong part of the foil paper, pulling the glittery gold off when she tried to move it. Wrinkling her nose, she glared at the package, then glanced at the eagle-eyed customer who'd now taken to finger tapping to show her displeasure.

Oops.

"That'd be the same person whose idea it was to try out her hot and horny holiday meal last night and isn't sharing how it went," Kathy said, her voice escalating from whisper to hiss loud enough to garner shopper attention.

Her face on fire, Pandora gave a hiss of her own.

"Shh. I'll share. Later," she promised as she gave in to the finger-tapping pressure and started the wrapping all over. "Now, help me with this ribbon, okay?"

"No." Kathy straightened, keeping her hold-the-ribbon fingers hostage and giving Pandora a stubborn look.

"Pandora, the gossip grapevine is running amok," Laurie, a waitress from the nearby diner, said as she approached the counter with a basketful of holiday shopping. "Lacy Garner claimed Caleb Black was in here flirting up a storm the other day. But Jolene Giamenti was telling everyone and their neighbor that Sheriff Kendall was interested in you. Now I'm dying of curiosity—which of those fine-looking gentlemen are you interested in?"

Pandora's lips curved as she wondered how to answer that. She'd never had two eligible men interested in her, and definitely never had the town gossiping over which one she'd choose. Her ego, starting to show its fragile face again, glowed a little at the idea.

"Which one?" repeated the finger-tapping Mrs. Vincent, giving a nod of approval for the wrapping and indicating that Pandora hurry up with a little wiggle of her fingers. "As if there could be a question. A sweet girl like Pandora is going to date our fine sheriff. Why would she have any interest in a hoodlum like Caleb Black? Of course, all three Black kids were wild. But Caleb, being the oldest, seemed to make a point of being the best troublemaker, too. Why would Pandora date someone like that?"

Why? For fourteen orgasms in one night, maybe? Or the soft sweetness of the kiss he'd brushed over her forehead before he'd left in the wee hours of the morning? Maybe because Caleb had a sense of humor almost as fine as his gorgeous body. Or that he was fun and entertaining and made her feel amazingly sexy and clever.

Pandora shifted from one foot to the other. The movement brushed her thighs together and instantly shot tingling little reminders of her wild night through her body. She shivered. She didn't regret for one second the evening that had led to such pleasure. But still, she needed to keep her professional persona intact. It didn't matter that this was her own sex life and as such, nobody else's nosy business. Just as it hadn't mattered that she was innocent in the debacle with Sean. She'd learned the hard way how easy it was for public opinion to destroy a career.

"Are you going to share, or aren't you?" Kathy prodded, snatching the package and tying the bow herself with a quick, sassy flick of her fingers. "I have a lot to do today. My mother wants to go shopping for matching Christmas sweaters, then I have to take the dog to the photographer to reshoot the holiday card."

"You know if you had cats, those cards would come out a lot better," Pandora pointed out, taking the package back, bagging it and handing it to Mrs. Vincent with a smile. "Cats are great at lying still."

She, Kathy and the two customers all looked toward Bonnie and Paulie, who were curled up together in the window, a picture of furry contentment on the alpaca throw displayed there.

"So what's going on?" Mrs. Vincent prodded, taking her bag but not leaving like a polite customer who minded her own business should. "Are you associating with that riffraff, Caleb Black? I hear he's been a huge stress to his daddy. Not that Tobias Black is a pillar of all that is good and right in the world, what with dating girls his daughter's age, those motorcycle types in and out of his shop and the constant traffic of questionable personalities. But he deserves better than a do-nothing son like that boy."

"Caleb isn't a do-nothing, Mrs. Vincent," Pandora defended, seeing the trap an instant too late.

"Guess that answers our question, then, doesn't it," Mrs. Vincent said with a wicked smile on her benign old-lady face. She and Mrs. Sellers hooked arms and sashayed out of the store, whispering and tossing dire looks back over their shoulders.

Another customer, one who Pandora didn't know personally, gave a judgmental sort of tut-tut, then went back to her shopping.

Panic gripped a tight fist in Pandora's stomach. What had she done? She should have kept things with Caleb quiet. The mess with Sean had been horrible, but the whispers and snide innuendo from everyone who knew them, everyone she'd worked with, that'd almost been worse.

"Pandora, I love what you've done here," a pretty blonde interrupted as she carried a large statue of Eros, the god of love to the counter. She patted his naked ceramic butt before pointing to the tower of boxed aphrodisiac pepper cookies, the day's special. "Can you throw in a box of extraspicy cookies, too? I think they'll be a perfect gift for my Jazzercise instructor."

"She likes cookies?" Kathy asked, apparently not in such a hurry that she didn't have time to be social. She leaned forward on the counter, trying to peek up Eros's flowing strip of fabric to see how he was hanging.

"Sure. But mostly it's because she's got this new boyfriend

and wants to make sure this relationship has a chance," the woman said, adding an astrology book, two CDs and a woven celestial shawl to the counter. "I guess she was dating this guy last month who was all about a little chemical enhancement, if you know what I mean. He claimed it'd boost their sex lives and make her look and feel gorgeous."

Starting to ring up the fabulous sale, Pandora exchanged a confused look with Kathy. Before she could ask, though, the woman continued. "She wasn't having anything to do with that fake stuff, though. But now she's paranoid that her new guy thinks she's ugly and that she sucks in bed. So I figured some cookie encouragement, along with a spa gift certificate, might help boost her confidence a little."

"Cookie courage," Pandora intoned with a wise nod.

The three of them joked their way through the rest of the transaction, but as soon as the door bells rang behind the blonde, Pandora frowned at Kathy.

"What do you think she's talking about? Chemical enhancements? Like…" She trailed off, then shrugged. "What do you think she meant?"

Kathy gave her a long, knowing look that clearly said she realized this was a pathetic topic change and she was allowing it for now. But there would be a price to pay. Pandora figured she'd better bring chocolate.

"Well, chemical usually means drugs," Kathy pointed out finally. Pandora nodded. "But the looking-good part? Maybe that means hallucinogens or something? Who knows?"

The two women shared a puzzled look.

"Pandora, did you want to open the café early today?" Fifi asked as she hurried from the back where she'd been prepping the cash register for lunch.

"We don't start serving until eleven," Pandora said, glancing at the clock shaped like a cat wearing a wizard hat. Most of the food was already prepped and ready in the kitchen, but she still needed to put the finishing touches on the asparagus salad and whip a fresh bowl of cream. "That's an hour away."

"I know, but I've had three people ask if we'd consider it. They need to be other places but really want your saffron chicken special."

"It'd be cool to bump up our income with an extra hour of lunch," Pandora mused, glancing at the beaded doorway leading to the café. "But I don't think we can. The store is too busy, I can't afford for one of us off the floor that much longer."

"Maybe we should hire holiday help?" Fifi said, her voice lifting in excitement. "I mean, even if it's only for the holidays. Things are so busy now, we could use another set of hands. I have a friend who'd be great. Russ. You've met him, right? He could come in during café hours. Maybe just until the new year when things slow down again?"

Hire help? Pandora bit her lip. What did she know about choosing employees? Fifi had worked at the store off and on for years, so it hadn't been as if Pandora had hired her so much as rehired her. But someone totally new? With her lousy judgment in people? She shuddered.

"You remember Russ? Kinda geeky guy who's been hanging around the store the last few weeks. He's a nice guy. Sweet and great at math," Fifi prodded. "Want me to give him a call?"

Pandora took a deep breath, looking around again. Her stomach was churning and she wanted to go hide in the office, make a list of pros and cons and debate the idea for a few hours.

But Fifi and Kathy were giving her expectant looks, and she had a store to run.

"Sure," she decided. Then realizing that she needed to be a businesswoman, not a wimp, she added, "I'll talk to him and see if I think he'd fit in well here at Moonspun Dreams."

"Oh, I think he will. He's fascinated by all things mystical and really wants to learn," Fifi said with an excited clap of her hands. "And he knows a lot of people. So I'm sure he'll be talking up the store and how great you're doing here, too."

Great, Pandora thought. Someone else talking about her. Just what she needed.

CALEB STRETCHED OUT on his hotel bed, staring in satisfaction at his stockinged feet. When the hell was the last time he'd taken a nap, let alone lounged around without his boots on?

Always being properly shod was a necessary component of always being ready to run. And he'd spent the past eight years, hell, his entire life, actually, ready to hit the road at a moment's notice.

A job gone wrong. A drugged-out dealer breaking in to kill him. A fight with one of his siblings. One of his dad's cons turning sour. All required footwear.

Wasn't it just a little ironic that the first taste he'd had of the ultimate deliciousness that was Pandora, he'd had his boots on? Or maybe it was some kind of cosmic payback for all his years of running.

He was still grinning a sappy, dork-ass grin when his cell rang.

"Black," he answered.

"Report?"

"Happy holidays, Hunter. How's the shopping coming along? Do you feebies do the secret Santa thing? Or do you buy for the entire task force? If so, don't forget my favorite color is gray."

"Not black?"

"Too obvious."

"Something you never are."

"Exactly."

"Are we finished?"

Caleb considered the white cotton of his stocking-clad toes for a few seconds, then nodded.

"Yep, sure. We're finished. What's up?"

"I'm calling for your status report."

"Is this how you handle your minions? Formal report requests? This businesslike tone that says, 'Dude, I'm in charge!'?"

"Is this how you talk to your superiors? With total disregard for authority? Your smart-ass mouth running on fast-forward?"

Caleb wiggled his toes, then nodded. "Yep. Guess that's why they aren't crying too hard over me retiring, huh?"

"I have trouble believing you actually think you can retire," Hunter said, now sounding more like Caleb's old roommate and beer buddy than an uptight FBI agent. "You're an adrenaline junky. You might be sick of the streets, but you're not going to be able to give up the job. Not totally."

Caleb's toes weren't looking so appealing anymore. Tension, as familiar as his own face, shot through his shoulders as he swung his feet to the floor.

"I could get used to not having people shoot at me. I'm thinking I'd like a life spent not dealing with strung-out hookers and South American drug lords with their zombie army of addicts."

"You'd just let them all go free?"

"I'm not the only guy out there, Hunter. There're plenty of DEA agents who can bring them down."

"As good as you?"

"Of course not."

Neither of them were kidding, Caleb knew. Hunter, because he didn't know how. And himself, because, well, he *was* damn good. But that didn't mean he wasn't finished.

"What'd you call for?" he asked, not willing to keep circling the same useless point he'd already discussed with his boss four times since he'd hit Black Oak for his fake vacation.

"Just what I said. I'm calling for your report."

"No, you're not. You're not a micromanager. If I had something to report, I'd have called you myself. And you know that. So what's the deal?"

The other man's hesitation was a physical thing. If he'd been in the room, Caleb knew he'd see the calculation in his old friend's eyes as he decided the best way to handle the situation. Good ole Hunter, always strategizing.

"Your father has some odd activity going on. A lot of major part orders, hiring a couple guys with dealing records, parties in the shop after hours."

Stonefaced, Caleb analyzed that info as objectively as possible. Then he shrugged. "It's the holidays—from what I've heard, he has a lot of big holiday orders. He probably needs mechanics to meet them, and isn't that picky about their backgrounds."

"He's dating some hottie in town. She was in your sister's graduating class."

Wincing, Caleb hunched his shoulders. Just when he thought his father couldn't embarrass him anymore…

"So my old man is snacking on a Twinkie. So what?"

"You know sex is one of the prime motivators. Have you checked this woman out?"

"I'm not checking out my father's old lady."

In the first place, the idea was gross. In the second, it would up the chances that he'd actually have to speak with his father. In the week he'd been in town, he'd managed to duck the guy's calls and avoid actually being in the same breathing space. He was calling it deep undercover. So deep, he wasn't even coming into contact with the suspect.

"She's the stepdaughter of a known South American

dealer. She's reputed to be estranged from her family, but the connection can't be ignored."

"Lilah Gomez?"

God, this was like some twisted soap opera. Striding over to the window, Caleb shoved his hand through his hair. This day had started out so nice. Incredible sex, a woman who filled his head with crazy thoughts of tomorrow and, dammit, relaxing in his stocking feet.

"You know her?"

He wasn't about to admit that after that first day when he hadn't recognized her, she'd gone on to hit on him three more times since he'd come to town. He grimaced. Especially since that he didn't know if her thing with his father was new or not.

"She and my sister were tight growing up. They hung out, had sleepovers, that kind of thing. Then Lilah went over to the wild side, and she and Maya went their separate ways."

Caleb waited, but Hunter didn't say anything about Lilah's current sleepover choices. And that, friends, was why he was still Caleb's best buddy.

"Look, I'm sorry," Hunter said instead.

Staring out the window at the frosty cold coating the bare tree branches, Caleb grunted.

"I'd hoped you'd find someone else. Another suspect or connection."

"Even if my old man's acting like a hound dog, there's still nothing to tie him to this," Caleb argued.

"There's nothing to point the finger in any other direction," Hunter rebutted. "Is there?"

Caleb sighed. "The case is moving slow. I've been connecting my way up the food chain. I'm cozying up to one of the midlevel dealers. He knows names, clearly has the inside track. But he's not sharing. Yet."

"Any hint about who's on top?"

Caleb grimaced. "These guys are cocky, sure they are untouchable. So it's someone with pull. Someone who can influence the law."

He waited, but again, Hunter didn't take the obvious opening. Gotta love the guy.

"I saw one of the couriers last night from a distance. He's familiar. As soon as I figure out where I've seen him before, I'll have the break we need."

"You've seen him on another case?"

Caleb thought back to the brown shaggy hair, all he'd been able to identify from two blocks away. "No, he's local. I'll do the rounds again, figure it out."

"Good job," Hunter said. "In the meantime, I have a remote, wildly impossible thread that if tugged could disintegrate instantly."

"Sounds promising."

He could handle delicate. Hell, if it meant keeping his old man out of jail, he could handle delicate while juggling porcelain and wearing roller skates.

"Intel shows that a new citizen to Black Oak has some connections. A relationship with a pharmacist busted for a prescription scam. She was implicated but skated."

"So why are you grudging after my old man? Why aren't you pounding on her door instead?"

"In the first place, it's not a grudge. Your old man has a record longer than I am tall."

"A record of suspicions. No convictions."

"Minor detail."

"Major legality."

"Whatever," Hunter dismissed. "And in the second place, while there is enough here to warrant a first glance, it's pretty much a waste of a second look. Other than this one relationship, the woman has a spotless rep. No record, no connections, no history to support drug suspicions."

"Once is all it takes." Especially if that once was the hook he needed to prove his old man's innocence. Just because he had issues with his upbringing, a lack of respect for his father's choices and a whole lot of pent-up anger toward the past, that didn't mean he wanted the old man in jail.

"Look, give me the name and I'll look into it," he told Hunter.

Even though the sigh was silent, Caleb knew his friend heaved one. Patience with avoidance had never been the guy's strong suit.

"Fine. Check on a Pandora Easton. I'll email you the deets of her record."

Sucker punched, stars swirled in front of his eyes as he tried to catch his breath. Caleb had been in bed with a pole dancer once, both of them buck naked and sweaty, when she'd pulled a gun on him. To this day, he had no idea where it'd come from.

That's about how he felt at this moment.

"Pandora…"

"Easton," Hunter confirmed. "Twenty-seven, resident of Black Oak and employed at a store there. Her mother, Cassiopeia Easton, has a file. I'll send that, too."

A part of Caleb's brain heard and filed away the details of Hunter's words. The rest of it was in shock.

Pandora? The sweetest woman he'd ever met? The one who'd shown him heaven by the lights of her Christmas tree, blown his control all to hell while giving him the best orgasm of his life? With his damn boots on?

Suddenly, busting his father for running a drug ring held a sort of appeal.

He'd spent hours in that store. Days watching it. He hadn't suspected her for one second. Now this? Unless he'd seriously lost his edge, this was all bullshit. Or was it?

"I've gotta go," he said, cutting off whatever Hunter was

saying. He flicked the cell phone closed, shoved it in his pocket and grabbed his jacket. It wasn't until he had the door to his hotel room open he remembered that he didn't have any damn boots on.

There was irony in there somewhere.

Five minutes later, he was on his way. To do what, he wasn't sure. Something with Pandora. He wasn't sure if that something was along the lines of the naked, intense pleasure that he'd been contemplating an hour ago, or if it was because he didn't like being lied to. Zipping his jacket, the leather minimal defense against the cold, Caleb stepped out of the hotel lobby and onto the wide porch steps and almost ran into the body coming up the stairs.

"Excuse me," he muttered, sidestepping and patting his pockets for his bike keys.

"I was coming in to look for you."

Could this damn day get any worse?

Caleb glanced at the keys in his hand, briefly wishing they were his gun. He shoved the keys back in his pocket, eyeing the railing and the drop. Whether it was to jump or to toss someone over, he wasn't sure.

"Dad," he returned, his tone resigned. He kept one eye on the railing, though. Just in case.

He'd been unprepared that first day when he'd seen his father. Since then, he'd spent every minute prepared for this second encounter. Now, he could study the old man with objective eyes. Or at least without the resentment and irritation he'd been sporting.

Tobias Black stood straight and tall, like his sons. His black hair was showing a little gray in the sideburns, but was still as thick and unruly as ever. As a kid, Caleb had seen his father in everything from a three-piece suit with an ascot, to a repairman's coveralls, to surgical scrubs. A chameleon, Tobias had obviously taken to this new role as custom-bike shop owner like a fish to water. Biker boots, similar to Caleb's own, jeans and a leather jacket made up his work uniform.

"I've been waiting for you to come by the house. Or the shop. Either one," Tobias said, shifting to the left and blocking the stairs leading to escape. Caleb smirked, knowing he could take the railing at any time he wanted.

"I've been busy."

"Doing?"

Leaning against one of the porch columns, his arms crossed over his chest, Caleb's smirk widened.

"Tell me, son, why'd you come home? Clearly not to see family, so what's up?"

"I stopped by to see Aunt Cynthia yesterday."

"How is that old bat?"

"She had a lot of great things to say about you."

Tobias's smirk was an exact replica of his son's.

"I'll just bet she did. The woman is still trying to run me out of town. You'd think she'd give up after all this time, but no. That's why she ran for mayor, you know. To make my life hell."

If anyone else had said that, Caleb would have rolled his eyes and called them on their whiny persecution complex. But in this case, he knew Tobias was right. Cynthia Parker had made it her mission to make her late sister's husband's life hell whenever possible. His kids, she tolerated. But Tobias? Not even a little bit.

"I gotta say, even for a harpy, I had higher expectations of her, though," Tobias continued. "She's too busy glad-handing rich donors and getting her picture taken to take care of business, I guess."

Caleb knew the game. If he asked what business, he'd be agreeing to play. Con 101, get the mark to agree. To anything, even if it was only to agree to talk about the weather. And for a master like Tobias, all he needed was that agreement, and he'd win. Always.

So Caleb waited.

Tobias clearly knew what his oldest son was doing.

"I don't suppose you're interested in coming by the bike shop this evening? Big holiday bash, all the vendors, customers, hell, even a few strangers. Probably a few of your old school pals. Good times, food provided by that little sweetheart at Moonspun, booze from Mick's bar."

Caleb saw the trap. Hell, it had a big neon sign flashing a warning at him. But he couldn't stop himself.

"You're tight with Pandora, are you?" he asked.

"Tight? What're you implying? The girl's young enough to be my daughter."

"So's Lilah Gomez."

Tobias's grin widened. Nope, this was his game and he was setting the traps, not stepping in them.

"Girl's gonna be at the party," he said.

"Lilah?" Caleb returned, even though he knew who his father meant.

"Pandora. I heard you had dinner with her the other night. Hope you're not taking on more than you can handle there."

Caleb's stare was bland. He hadn't discussed his sex life with his father since he was twelve and the old man had shown him the hall closet where the supply of condoms was kept. He was hardly going to start now.

"There's a lot of interesting…stuff coming out of that store," Tobias continued. His blue eyes were intense, the same look Caleb often saw when he looked in the mirror.

"Define *interesting*," Caleb invited. He knew Tobias wouldn't—after all, why waste bait? But he wanted to see where his father was taking this.

"Come by tonight," Tobias invited with a nod. Apparently

Caleb had done something right—who the hell knew what—in the old man's eyes. "You might learn a few things."

With that and a jaunty salute, Tobias turned on his heel and sauntered down the stairs.

9

By SEVEN-THIRTY IN THE evening, Pandora was closing up the store and about ready to scream.

She'd thought she was having a little fun with the most incredible sex of her life. But according to popular thought in the store today, she was actually making a social statement that was quite possibly going to cast her as a pariah in town and ruin her reputation. Having played that role recently, she knew she pretty much hated it.

And, apparently the cherry on top of public opinion was that by choosing Caleb over Sheriff Hottie, she was rejecting all that was good and right in the world for the lure of the bad.

It was enough to make a girl's head explode right off her shoulders. But she knew from experience that obsessing didn't help, so she forced herself to start her closing routine.

It was just as well that Caleb hadn't come by. Or called. Or expressed any interest in a repeat performance. If one night together had the potential to ruin everything she'd built here, what would two nights do? Ruin it twice as much?

And how pathetic was she to stop and consider whether twice as ruined wasn't worth it. Because, dammit, the sex had been incredible. Mind-boggling. So awesome that she got damp just thinking about it.

And she knew he'd been just as blown away.

"Why the hell hasn't he called, then?" she muttered as she wheeled the dolly with its precariously balanced crate into the showroom.

She stopped just short of Paulie, who was splayed over the floor like a cat-skin rug, and wheeled the dolly to the right instead.

"I'm crazy for being upset. I should be grateful he isn't coming around, right? This way I don't have to worry about trying to resist him."

This time she directed her comment to Bonnie, who was sitting on one of the display counters next to a three-foot-high cluster of amethyst, her head tilted to the side as if contemplating Pandora's whining.

Bonnie meowed her support. But Paulie just rolled onto his side, shot one leg into the air and started licking himself. There was nothing like the male perspective.

"Sure, I guess he could take that route," she agreed with the cat as she started wiggling the five-foot-tall statue of Eros from the box, careful not to nick his wings. "But lovin' is never as fun by oneself."

Pandora's lower lip jutted out, but before she could get a real pout on, there was a tap at the door.

She and the cats all turned their heads. Her heart leaped, giddy excitement filling her tummy. Dread filtered in, too. She'd had no idea she was making a public statement last night. But now she was fully informed. Upset, confused and a little intimidated…but still fully informed.

Oh, joy.

Giving Eros's butt a quick pat in the hopes he'd help her choose well, she unwrapped herself from the statue and hurried across the store to unlock the door.

"Caleb," she greeted, her smile a little shaky at the corners. She wiped her hands on the heavy velvet of her skirt and gave her voile blouse a quick tug to make sure the lace was straight at the bodice.

Should she ask him in? Or ask him to leave? Her stomach churned as she tried to decide. Did she go with her instincts and intuition, which said that despite the town's opinion, he was a good man? Or did she accept that her intuition sucked and listen to public opinion?

Thankfully, Caleb took the decision out of her hands by walking right in.

"Hey," he greeted. He didn't kiss her, though. Instead, he gave her a long, searching look, then, hands still shoved in his pockets instead of groping her the way they should be, he stepped into the store.

"What's up?" she asked. She bit her lip. Had he heard the rumors about the two of them? Was he regretting it now, too? "You look a little stressed."

"Nah. I just had a full day, that's all."

Full of what? He wasn't working, was avoiding his family as if they were carriers of the seventh plague and didn't seem like a holiday-partying kind of guy.

Maybe he'd been looking for a job. Or a place to live. Something that'd keep him in Black Oak past the first of the year? Maybe he'd spent the day in bed, recovering in exhaustion from his wild night with her.

And maybe she'd been inhaling too many oyster fumes. Pandora gave herself a quick mental forehead smack, followed by an even quicker get-a-freaking-clue-he's-not-for-you lecture.

"I'm replenishing stock," she told him, returning to unpacking the statue so she could resist the desperate urge to squeeze his ass. Keep it light, keep it polite. Ass grabbing was definitely off-limits. "It was a busy day. The busiest this year, actually."

"That's great that you're rocking the sales," he said. "Have you pinpointed what's making the big difference? Besides your charming personality, of course."

The last was said with a wicked smile and a wink.

"I'm guessing it's either that, or the aphrodisiacs," Pandora said with a smile, unable to maintain her distance when he gave her that look. "I'm not actually sure. I haven't quite figured out how to run the bookkeeping program yet, but I think there's some kind of income-comparison report I can run. As soon as I do, I'll know what to focus more time on."

His eyes narrowed, an odd look crossing his face before he stepped farther into the room. "I'm handy with computers. How about I run the report for you while you unpack?"

"You don't have to do that," she protested, her words a little breathless. "I'm sure you have other things to do."

"Just the party at the motorcycle shop," he dismissed. "And I was hoping you'd go with me, so I'm just chilling until you're through here anyway."

Pandora pressed her lips together. Wasn't that tantamount to publicly stating her intention to take the bad-boy path?

"The party?" she hedged. "I didn't think you were going."

In that second, Pandora wished like never before that her mom were here. As conflicted as she felt, she needed Cassiopeia's clear-sighted vision and maybe a session with the tarot cards to sort through all of this.

Instead, she was stuck with herself. And her own lousy intuition. Tiny pinpricks of panic shivered up and down Pandora's spine as she tried to decide what to do. Her intuition was telling her to go for it with Caleb. Of course, her body's desperate need to taste him at least one more time was probably overriding any teensy bit of actual gift she had.

Obviously catching a whiff of her internal struggle, Caleb waved one hand as if brushing away the invitation.

"Look, I don't blame you if you don't want to go. It's not my idea of a good time," Caleb said with a shrug, moving behind the counter to where she'd left the laptop open. "What program do you use for bookkeeping?"

If they stayed here, she could enjoy his company and not have to face crowds. Or decisions. Oh, God, Pandora thought with a mental eye roll. She was such a wimp.

"You really don't have to do that," she said, feeling guilty over the relief. "I can come in early tomorrow and finish up the stock. We can go to the party now. Or, you know, go do something else."

Subtle, Pandora, she told herself with a mental snicker. Why didn't she ask him to drop his pants and do her instead?

"Nah," he said. "This won't take long and I'd like to help."

Her heart melted a little. So did her knees, so Pandora leaned against the dolly and cleared her throat, not wanting to sound all choked up when she said, "I appreciate it. I feel like I'm…"

She trailed off, scrunching her nose and scraping at the chipped paint on the dolly.

"Feel like…?"

Flustered and wishing she'd kept her mouth shut, Pandora met his gaze with a shrug.

"Pandora?"

"I feel like I've finally found my thing, you know? My niche. I'm having fun getting to know the customers and matching them to the right motivation." She blushed again, giving him an abashed look. "That's how I think of it. Motivation. What products will get them excited, give them the boost or direction they need. Even the aphrodisiacs in the café are all about motivation."

Pushing the dolly toward the back room, Pandora caught his doubtful look.

"They are," she insisted. "The aphrodisiacs aren't like popping a little blue sex pill and getting it up for anyone or anything. They're about amplifying a connection that's already there. About giving a couple the impetus, the energy, to lose their inhibitions and explore everything that's between them."

Caleb leaned against the counter, his fingers tapping the edge of the laptop as he smiled.

"You love it."

Centering her statue, Pandora rubbed Eros's bare shoulder and nodded. "I really do."

"Then let me help you out. I'll just take a peek at your program, see what info I can pull together for you."

Could anyone be sweeter? To hell with the town and the gossip. She was going to listen to her heart. It might not be a special gift like intuition or a honed skill like reading body language. But it was hers and she was going to trust it.

"I APPRECIATE YOU LOOKING at my books," Pandora said, her smile both sweet and sexy at the same time. She crossed the floor, pausing to pet one of the cats, who was sprawled inside a large copper bowl. "I figure I'll take a business class or something after the first of the year. But in the meantime, I really am grateful for the reassurance that the store is really doing well."

Caleb felt like the world's biggest dick. And not in a good way. He spent most of his life lying to people. Using them for information. He'd learned the art of taking advantage of people at his father's knee.

And now?

Now he was standing in front of a woman who made him feel things, believe in things that he'd always scoffed at as feel-good lies before. And he was bullshitting her, poking into her business while pretending to help her out. He was digging into her books trying to find the dirt to convict her of an ugly crime.

No, he corrected himself. He was assuring himself that there was no dirt, so she didn't get unfairly accused.

Big difference, he thought with a mental eye roll.

She reached the counter and hesitated, her smile dimming as she studied his face. A tiny crease marred her forehead and she took a little step back, as if to get a better view of him.

"Seriously. What's the matter? You're really tense and, well, off feeling," she said, studying him through suddenly narrowed eyes.

Caleb was impressed. He'd spent the past eight years working with career cops whose lives depended on their ability to read people. And most of them didn't come close to her aptitude.

"What's wrong?" she asked again, her voice rising to a squeak as she wrung her fingers together. "Is the store losing money and I didn't realize it?"

"No. I mean, I don't know, I haven't started poking into your books yet," he told her. Giving a quick flick of the mouse pad, he gestured. "I need your password to get into the program."

"Ooooh." She reached around, angling the laptop and tapping a few keys, then trailed her hand over the back of his. He felt tingles, freaking tingles, from his fingers to the tip of his dick. It was as if she had some special power or something.

"Have at it," she told him, offering another warm smile before turning back to her naked-angel statue and boxes of stuff. "There are cookies there in that box, too. Help yourself."

He glanced at the box of Decadently Orgasmic Double-Chocolate Delights. Homemade horny treats. Curious, he flipped the lid and tasted one.

Delicious.

As Pandora restocked, tidied and replenished the bookcases and swept the floor, she kept up a steady stream of chatter. Caleb was alternately intrigued, amused and filled with an alien sense of comfort.

All the while, he invaded her privacy in horrible and disgusting ways, poking into all her files, opening her emails and reading her OneNote journal of store plans. He scrolled through the photo album, he checked her recycle bin and he surreptitiously jotted down names and numbers. He also ate her entire box of cookies.

The only loose end he was seeing was Fifi, though. But as far as he knew, she'd been employed at Moonspun off and on for years. He'd dig deeper into her history later, but from what he'd seen in the reports Hunter sent, she had a few financial issues and had been caught with the wrong crowd from time to time. However, she had no record and no real criminal ties.

Done with the laptop, he closed the lid. And gave thanks that Pandora was one of those organized, ethical people who kept their work and private computers completely separate. Because her work computer was clean, and he hadn't had the opportunity—ie: had to force himself—to look through her private files. Poking into her private emails and photos would feel really grimy. As opposed to just slightly nauseating.

"So how's it looking?" she asked as she came out of the storeroom.

It?

His conscience? That was looking like shit.

But he figured she wasn't interested in that. And if he played his cards right, she never had to know that he was so far beneath her in terms of moral values that he should be eating worms.

"The store's doing great. I'm impressed at how low you

keep your overhead," he commented, bringing up the only area left that might offer an opening for drug sales through her store. Unrealistic, of course, but once he'd crossed it off the list, he could tell Hunter this was definitely a closed door.

"Overhead?"

"Yeah. You don't have a big employee list. Just you and Fifi, right?"

"Well, yeah. Until tomorrow."

"Beg pardon?"

"Fifi thought we were going a little crazy with how busy it's been. Without knowing exactly how solid we were financially, I wasn't sure about hiring, but she convinced me that her friend Russ would be willing to work just the lunch shift while the café is open, and that he was cool with the fact that the job will end after Christmas." She gave a little shoulder wiggle and added, "Isn't that lucky?"

Caleb sighed. Of course she'd hired someone. She, and Fifi, who had a maxed-out VISA card and rent issues.

"Yep. That's lucky, all right." Bad luck, though. While he hadn't found anything to point fingers, he couldn't in good conscience cross the store off, either. Not until he'd checked out everyone.

"I guess I need to figure out how to add him to the payroll program, don't I?" she asked, biting her lip and giving Caleb the cutest eyelash-batting look that just screamed pretty please.

"I can do that," he offered, feeling like ten times the jerk because she looked so grateful.

"His application is back in the storeroom," she said, hurrying around the counter and stepping over the blanket of black furry cat lying in the doorway.

Since he couldn't have manufactured a better excuse to poke around in her storeroom, no pun intended, Caleb sighed and followed her. The cat lifted his fluffy black head and gave Caleb a long, narrowed look that made him want to hunch his shoulders and apologize.

God, it was time to get out of this business. Now a cat was calling him out on his bullshit.

"This is a storeroom?" Caleb asked, his eyes wide as he stepped into the tiny room. It was maybe eight-by-eight, with shelves lining three walls, boxes stacked in what he assumed were organized piles and a desk shoved in the back.

With a little squeak, Pandora turned to face him. Hand pressed to her chest, she laughed at herself. "I didn't realize you'd followed me."

He knew he shouldn't be here. He knew it was every kind of wrong to pursue her when she was under investigation. But, dammit, he'd already had a taste and now he was addicted. She was delicious. And he wanted more.

Caleb tried to justify it. He told himself he wasn't officially on the job. He argued that he'd already investigated her enough to know she was clean.

It was all bullshit.

But it was still good enough for him.

"The view wasn't as nice without you out there."

He loved how the color warmed her cheeks, bringing out the red highlights in her hair and making her eyes sparkle even brighter.

"I like it in here," he commented, stepping into the tight space and crowding her against the desk.

"Cassiopeia used this as an office," she said, gesturing over her shoulder to indicate the desk and file cabinet. She sounded a little breathless, though. Good. He liked the idea of taking her breath away. "She, um, she stored most of the stock in the back room. But, you know, I turned it into the café."

Her eyes were huge, so huge he could see the brown rim around the green irises. Her lashes, thick and black, swept down to hide her eyes. But he'd seen the desire in those hazel depths. Which was all the permission he needed.

Caleb took that last step. The one that brought his body within inches of hers. Hot, welcoming and so freaking soft she made his head spin, her curves melded into the hard planes of his chest.

Pandora tilted her head back so her hair swept over his wrists. Her hands slipped over his shoulders and she gave him a saucy wink.

"So you like tight spaces, do you?"

And just like that, his brain short-circuited. Caleb knew he was on the job here—even if he wasn't exactly 'on the job.' He knew there was a specific purpose to his being in this office, which was to find proof that would eliminate Pandora from suspicion so he could go back to happily enjoying the delights of her company without guilt. He should be looking for the job application so he could eliminate the new guy as a suspect.

But all he could see was Pandora, her hazel eyes laughing up at him. Her smile, so wide and amused. Her. Just her.

When had she gained so much power over him?

He had to get the hell out of here. Years of living on the edge of his nerves had honed his awareness razor-sharp. He knew when he was in trouble. He knew when he was in danger. And he knew when things had the potential to get freaking scary.

This situation? It was all three.

"Are you hungry?" Pandora asked, running her tongue over the fullness of her lower lip. "Did you want another... cookie?"

He didn't think she meant those delicious chocolate treats he'd eaten earlier. But he didn't care any longer. All he wanted was her. She was worth whatever problems he had to face—on the case, or with his conscience.

"I'm starving," he said. Then he gave in to the desperate need and skimmed his fingers down to gather the material of her skirt. Inch by inch, he pulled it higher, baring the deliciously soft skin of her thighs. "Another round with my boots on?"

"It's going to have to be, since I don't think you're going to have time to take them off," she mused, trailing her hands down to his belt buckle and having her way with it.

Her mouth met his with fervor, her tongue challenging his. She had his jeans unzipped and his dick free before he could do more than groan.

Suddenly desperate, he grasped her waist and lifted her onto the desk. His fingers found her wet, hot core, stroking her through the soft fabric of her panties. Impatient, needing more, he ripped the material away.

Her response was half laugh, half moan. And all delight.

Not sure he could stand much more of her fingers' wicked dance over his straining erection, he grabbed a condom from his pocket and sheathed himself.

His fingers returned to her soft folds, but she wasn't having any of that foreplay crap. Pandora grasped his hips, slid forward on the desk and rotated her hips so her wet heat stroked him.

Losing his mind, Caleb plunged.

It felt incredible. Her body, the power of the passion between them, the need.

Desperate for release, his eyes locked on Pandora's as he pounded into her. She didn't look away. Even as her eyes fogged, as she panted and started keening excited cries of her orgasm, she kept her gaze on his.

It was the most incredible experience of his life. Passionate, raw and emotional.

Terrified and exhilarated at the same time, he gave himself over to the pleasure of her body. His orgasm slammed him hard, exploding out of control. He shouted his pleasure, then, his face buried in the sweet scent of her shoulder, he tried to catch his breath. And restart his brain.

Because while he might not have a clue what he was going to do about the case, he did know one thing for damn sure.

He was in trouble.

And he liked it.

Ten minutes later, Caleb still couldn't think straight. He'd barely had the presence of mind to slip that job application in his pocket while she wasn't looking. He could check into the new employee later, then slip it behind the desk tomorrow. She'd never know.

"Thanks for the, um, help with my books," Pandora said with a laugh as she gathered her purse, keys and coat in preparation for closing up shop for the night.

He held her long suede coat so she could slide her arms into the sleeves.

"Ready to party?" he said, lifting the silky swing of her hair aside so he could brush a kiss over the back of her neck. God, he couldn't get enough of her. She was like a drug, addicting and delicious. And as far as he could tell, without any debilitating side effects.

"I have to say I feel a little weird going to a party with no undies," she said with a naughty glance over her shoulder. "Even weirder when it's your dad's party."

He wanted to tell her they'd skip it. He'd much rather go back to her place. Or to his hotel room with that big claw-foot tub. He wasn't a foofy bath kind of guy, but he could totally imagine Pandora lounging there, surrounded by steam and frothy bubbles.

But he had a job to do. He'd identified most of the dealers in town by now, so he needed to see if any showed up. And find out who they were hanging out with if they were there.

"We'll just stop in. Thirty minutes, tops," he said. That's

all he'd need to gauge the players and gather a few names. "And if we're there too long, all you have to do is whisper in my ear a reminder of your lack of panties, and we'll be out the door in an instant."

Pandora's laugh was low and husky, making him wish like hell that he could toss this whole mess aside and just focus on getting on with his damn life.

As soon as this case was solved, he was through. He had no clue what he'd be doing. He didn't even know where he'd be doing it, although Black Oak offered some serious temptation. Not quite enough to allay the issues it presented, though.

"You sure you don't want to just skip the party and get right to the lack of panties," Pandora said, only sounding as if she was half teasing as she gathered her purse and gave the cats each a cuddle.

"I want to," he said in an embarrassingly fervent tone. Caleb coughed, trying to clear the dorkiness from his throat. "It sounds crazy, but I feel like I have to stop in. I can't figure out what I'm doing until I figure out where things are at with my father. Not just for tonight, but in the big picture, you know."

Pandora paused in the act of pulling catnip-filled toys out a little mesh bag and tossing them around the room for Paulie and Bonnie to entertain themselves through the night. "Big picture?"

"Yeah." Caleb felt like an ass, but still something forced him to say, "I figure it's time we made our peace. Or at least found some neutral ground. See if we can both handle being in the same town for a length of time."

An earless furry bunny dangling from one hand, Pandora pressed the other to her lips for just a second, as if she was trying to hold back a slew of questions. There was just as much worry and hesitation in her eyes as there was curiosity and delight. He wasn't quite sure what to make of that.

"By length of time, do you mean the week left until Christmas?" she asked hesitantly.

While she waited, her eyes all huge and sexy, Bonnie, the black-and-white cat, padded across the floor and started batting the bunny with her paw. When Pandora didn't respond to the command to play, the cat batted harder, sending the toy flying from Pandora's fingers across the room. Both cats bounded after the furry treat.

"I'm…" He trailed off. How did he answer? He didn't want to get her hopes up. He wasn't the kind of guy who made promises. Not even ones he was pretty sure he could keep.

"Don't," she said, interrupting his mental struggle. She crossed over and took his hands. "Please, I didn't mean to make you uncomfortable. I should warn you, though, that the town grapevine is working overtime and you're the main topic. So if you stay, that's only going to get worse."

It wasn't the town he needed to worry about, he realized as he looked into those heavily fringed eyes. It was Pandora. She was more dangerous than an arsenal of AK-47s. At least, she was to his once happily frozen heart.

"Sweetheart, I honestly don't know where I'm going to be, or where I want to be, in two weeks. But I do know I'm exactly where I want to be right this minute."

Pandora's eyes were huge and vulnerable. He'd like to think it was because of his heartfelt declaration. But there was something else there, lurking. Something that made his gut clench. Because beneath the nerves and sweetness there was a fear. Like she was afraid of him sticking for too long. Afraid of what he'd find out.

"Pandora?" he prodded. "Is there something you want to tell me?"

He didn't know if he was hoping more that she would, or that she wouldn't.

"You're exactly where I want you to be, too," she finally

murmured. Whether that was true or not, he didn't know. But he was positive it wasn't what she'd been thinking about.

But before he could push, she rose on tiptoe, and, even as nerves simmered in her eyes, brushed a soft kiss over his lips.

It was as if she'd flipped a switch that only she knew existed. His body went on instant hard-on alert, and his mind absolutely shut down. All he wanted was her. All he could taste, could think of, cared about, was her.

More and more of her.

He slanted his mouth to the side, taking their kiss deeper with one swift slide of his tongue.

His fingers still entwined with hers, Caleb let his hands drop, then wrapped both their arms around her waist to pull her tighter, effectively trapping her soft curves against the hard, craving planes of his body.

Why the hell was she wearing this bulky coat? All he wanted, now and for as long as it lasted, was to get her naked.

Lost in the pleasure of her mouth, Caleb didn't hear the key in the door until a loud clatter of the chimes hit a discordant note. Pulling her lips from his, Pandora jumped, blinking the sexual glow out of her eyes as she looked over his shoulder toward whoever had come in.

Her jaw dropped and her face turned bright red even as embarrassment filled her eyes.

"Hello, Mother."

10

"WELL, DARLING?" Cassiopeia said as she settled comfortably on Pandora's couch and sipped chamomile tea. "It looks like you have a lot to share. When did you get involved with the likes of Caleb Black? And more important, why didn't you ever mention him in your emails? I'd have stayed away a few extra days if I'd known you had that kind of entertainment on tap."

That entertainment, as Cassiopeia called him, had barely stuck around long enough for introductions before he'd hightailed it out of the store for his father's party.

Now, twenty minutes after Cassiopeia's shocking arrival, she was soothing her travel woes with tea while Pandora resisted the urge to pace.

"I've got so much to tell you. I shared the basics in our emails, but things are really going great at the store," she said, even as a part of her wondered if she hurried her mother along, could she catch Caleb at the party. The other part of her, the one that bwawked like a chicken, was glad her mother's arrival had given her an excuse to keep their relationship quiet for a little longer. Sort of. Nothing was ever hidden from Cassiopeia.

As if reading her mind, her mother gestured with her teacup.

"I'd rather talk about the man," Cassiopeia said with a smile too wicked for someone's mother.

"I'd rather not," Pandora decided. Not while she was so mixed up over the issue. "Let's focus on the store instead, okay? Before we left, I printed out the financial statements. Do you want to see them? I saved the store, Mom."

She felt a little giddy saying that. As if she was tempting fate. But she was so excited she had to share. And hoped, like crazy, that her mom would be proud.

"I mean, it's obviously too early to tell for sure, but I'm betting the café and the aphrodisiacs stay solid, long-term."

"Most likely," Cassiopeia agreed with a shrug that seemed more disinterested than dismissive.

"Don't you care?" Pandora frowned, trying to read her mother. Calm and centered, as always. A little worn-out, which wasn't surprising since it was a long trip from Sedona. But shouldn't there be some relief? Some joy at the prospect of keeping the store a success? Some pride in her only child?

"Darling, of course I care. The café is a brilliant idea and you've done a wonderful job. I knew if left to your own devices, you'd come up with something."

Her mother's smile widened, a self-satisfied look just this side of gloating in her eyes.

"You left to force my hand?" Pandora realized, almost breathless from the shock.

"Well, the store *was* in trouble, of course. And I was having a heck of a time figuring out how to keep things afloat and still meet my commitment in Sedona. But I imagine I could have probably muddled through, canceled the appearance and crossed my fingers until the spring bus tour if I'd had to." Cassiopeia waved a heavily bejeweled hand as if her manipulation didn't matter. "But the point is, I didn't have to. Thanks to your return to Black Oak, and your clever café idea, we're in wonderful shape for the first time in years."

"That was a huge risk to take if you didn't have to," Pandora pointed out, trying to calm her sudden jitters. "I could have ruined the store. What if I'd failed?"

"Then you'd fail," Cassiopeia said with a shrug.

"You'd risk the family legacy to teach me a lesson?"

"The family legacy is talent, dear. It's intuition. It's not a building and a bunch of candles and crystals."

Pandora choked down the urge to scream. She knew what the hell to do with the shop, dammit. But she didn't have any talent. So where did that leave her? She'd thought she'd finally contributed to the family name. That she'd done something worthy of the women who'd come before her.

"Darling, you make it so hard on yourself. Instead of embracing hope, which will help you realize your gift, you spend all your time chasing the Furies, trying to corral misery before it causes hurt," Cassiopeia said, launching into one of her favorite stories. In the Easton family, they didn't believe in choosing a name until they'd discovered the newborn's personality. Pandora had been Baby Girl for eight months until the gods, fate and the tarot cards had revealed her destiny to Cassiopeia. "You need to quit worrying about those miseries, darling. Instead, focus on joy. That's the only way you'll find the right path."

With that, Cassiopeia rose and glided to the kitchen to set her teacup in the sink, returned to kiss the top of her silently fuming daughter's head and left.

An hour later, frustrated tears still trickled down Pandora's cheeks. She didn't even answer when someone knocked tentatively on her door. Eleven o'clock on a Sunday night, it could only be one person. And she was too worked up to deal with her mother twice in one day.

The knock sounded again, a little louder this time.

Who the hell needed to chase misery when it was always right there, tapping her on the shoulder and reminding her that she didn't measure up. That she was a waste of her family name. Ungifted and unworthy.

The urge to run away—again—made her body quiver. But unlike her escape when she'd been eighteen, this time she didn't have anywhere to go. Nor did she still have that cocky faith that she could prove to her mother, her grandmother and everyone else in Black Oak that she could be a success without the family gift.

Pounding replaced the tentative knock.

"Fine," she huffed, jumping to her feet.

Her mother wouldn't give up. She had probably headed home to gather some crystals and cards, determined to help her daughter find that damned path she always harped on.

"What?" Pandora snapped as she threw open the door.

The bitter cold from the icy rain swept over her bare toes as she stared.

"Oh."

It wasn't Cassiopeia on her doorstep.

It was a delicious looking chocolate éclair with what looked like a tub of ice cream and, if she wasn't mistaken, hot-fudge sauce.

Her eyes met Caleb's golden gaze.

"I thought you could use a sugar rush," he said, lifting the dessert a little higher. "It comes with, or without, a second spoon."

She hesitated. Attention was a good thing, but attention while she was having a tantrum? Hardly something she wanted Caleb to remember her for.

"I'm not very good company right now," she demurred, rubbing her hands over the velvet of her skirt and wishing she were wearing sweatpants and a baggy T-shirt. Something innocuous to hide behind. Although, if she was going to do some wishing, she should put all her falling stars and birthday candles toward having washed her tear-stained face instead of answering the door looking like a sad raccoon.

"I'm not looking for entertainment," Caleb said, shrugging before leaning one broad shoulder against the door frame. Catching the arch look she shot him, he grinned. "I'm not looking for that, either."

"Oh, really?"

"Well, I wouldn't say no if you decided to strip naked and paint my name across your body in this fudge sauce before inviting me to lick it off." He waited for Pandora's laugh before continuing, "But that's not what this is about. I'm just here as…as…"

Pandora swallowed hard to get past the lump of emotions suddenly clogging her throat. "As?"

"As a friend."

The only thing that kept the tears from leaking down her face was fear of adding another layer to the raccoon effect. Instead, Pandora sniffed surreptitiously and stepped aside to let him in.

"How'd you know I needed a friend tonight?" she asked as Caleb crossed the room. "Better yet, how'd you know my mother wasn't still here?"

"She stopped by the party." He gave her a quick look, something shuttered in his eyes making her wonder if he'd had his own parental confrontation. "She looked a little stressed herself, so I figured I'd check on you."

So Cassiopeia had decided to skip the crystals and cards and had sent in a sexy ego boost instead. Too dejected to even fake being a good hostess, Pandora dumped two bowls on the table. Caleb, jacket gone and his shirtsleeves rolled up, scooped big fat mounds of vanilla-bean ice cream into them.

Her frustration and hurt feelings shifted, sliding into second place behind her sudden urge to lick hot fudge off his knuckle. Her body warmed, excitement stirring at the sight of Caleb's hands. So strong. So big. So wonderfully good at sending her into a fog of desire where she could forget everything except him and the pleasure he brought.

"What?" he said, noting her stare.

"Just realizing something," she said, color warming her cheeks.

"Again… What?"

"You have magic hands," Pandora admitted despite her embarrassment. "I knew they felt incredible. I've had plenty of proof of their copious talents. But I didn't realize until just now that they are magic."

Caleb's grin was huge as he plopped sloppy globs of whipped cream on top of the fudge-covered ice cream. "Magic, huh?"

"Yep." Pandora pulled one of the bowls toward her, grabbing a spoon with the other hand.

She suddenly felt a million times better.

"Tell me more," he invited, stashing what was left of dessert in the freezer. He joined her at the table, but didn't sit.

"More, hmm?" she said, giving him a slow, teasing smile as she licked hot fudge off her spoon. The rich, bittersweet flavor slid down her throat. "How about we make it a show-and-tell kind of thing?"

His wicked smile didn't change, but his eyes did. They sharpened and heated at the same time. He reached out a hand, pulling her to her feet. Then he scooped up his bowl, handing her the other one, and led the way out of the kitchen.

"We're eating in bed?" she teased as excitement spun and swirled like a snowflake inside her, buffeting through her system and making her breathless with need.

"Too messy," he deemed, continuing through the living room, one hand wrapped around hers to keep her close. He stopped at the bathroom and glanced in, gave a decisive nod, then turned to her with an arched brow. "Do you have a blanket you don't mind getting sticky?"

"Sticky?"

"Babe, even if I paint as carefully as I can, my magic hands might drip a little bit before I can lick this hot fudge off your naked body."

"That's going to make a mess," she said, not really caring.

"That's what bubble bath is for," he assured her. "I assume you have bubbles."

Bubbles?

Ten minutes ago she'd been wallowing in misery, sure her life sucked hard. And now? Now she had Caleb, with his tub of vanilla ice cream, his gorgeous smile and an intuitive understanding of her that nobody, not even her best friend, had ever had.

He made her feel so many things. Sexual and passionate. Exciting and fun. Brave and strong and interesting.

But most of all, he made her feel safe. Like it was okay to stand in the middle of the room and make a fool of herself. Like he accepted and appreciated her. All of her.

And now he wanted to feed her dessert, then take a bubble bath with her. Yes, it was sexual. But she knew it was more than that. She could see it in his body language. In the set of his shoulders and the concern on his face.

He was doing it to make her feel better.

"I do have bubbles," she said, trying not to giggle at the image of the ultramasculine Caleb Black surrounded by frothy floral-scented bubbles.

And from the terrified nerves jumping through her system at her realization. She was in love with him.

That wasn't the plan. It was crazy. It was a huge mistake. And she didn't care. She wasn't going to let herself. Not right now. It might not be her path, but it was a wonderful place to

be. And just for now, she was going to give herself the gift
of enjoying it.

"And I'll be happy to share my bubbles with you," she assured him as she grabbed a blanket off the couch and laid it
in front of the Christmas tree. "Right after we find out who
can get whom stickier."

"YOU SMELL LIKE FLOWERS," Fifi observed as Pandora swept
into the store the next day. "Is that a new perfume?"

"Bubble bath," she told the blonde, winking. "I'm going
to get started on the cookies and desserts for today's lunch
crowd, okay? Can you handle the store yourself?"

"Russ is in soon, I'll be fine," Fifi assured her.

Pandora winced. She'd forgotten Russ was starting today.
Adding that to her to-do list, she headed back to the café and
its tiny kitchen. As she went, though, she heard the whispers
start.

Like a wave, the words flowed toward her, softly at first,
then crashing in a big splash. *Caleb Black. Dumped the poor
sweet sheriff. What could she be thinking? Poor mother, had
to come home to fix it.*

Pandora's feet froze on the threshold of the café. A part
of her wanted to turn around and face the gossips. To insist
they say it to her face so she could refute their words. The
rest of her wanted to run into the back room as fast as she
could, tugging her hair as she went to relieve the pressure on
her brain.

She wasn't going to think about it, she decided as she
forced her feet to move. She couldn't. Her mother had told
her to choose a path and this was the one she was on. She
was in love with Caleb Black. And if that meant dealing with
gossip, then she'd deal.

Washing her hands, she let the water trickle over her skin,

warming her and easing the tension. Eyes closed, she took some deep breaths and tried to center herself.

Out the kitchen window, a movement caught her eye. Three scruffy-looking guys were arguing in the alley. She frowned, realizing one of them was Russ. What was he doing back there?

Then one of them took a swing at another. She gasped, stepping back and cringing. Before she could go get the phone to call Tobias for help, a fourth guy waded in.

Pandora's heart calmed. Sheriff Kendall. He'd deal with it. Remembering her mother's warning about chasing miseries, she turned away. She didn't want to see, hear or experience anything else that stirred up tension, so she ignored the rest of the drama and got to work. She had cookies to bake, sandwiches to prep and éclairs to pipe.

An hour later, she was still in her Zen mood as she arranged half the cookies on a large silver platter and the others in to-go boxes.

"Darling, this is wonderful," her mother drawled as she swept into the tiny kitchen, mingling the scent of peanut butter and chocolate with the aroma of Chanel and the nag champa incense she always burned at home. "I love the ambience. And these tables are so adorable. It's so clever, the way you've used the red soy candles in the dish of rose quartz. Love and lust, with just enough liking to keep things from getting sticky, hmm?"

Her Zen shot all to hell, Pandora just shrugged. She knew she was pouting like a brat, but she didn't want to face her mother yet. She'd been happily distracted by Caleb. Incredible sex and the realization that she was falling in love was enough for any girl to handle for one morning, wasn't it?

"Darling, don't be in a snit. You came home for a reason, didn't you?" As soon as Pandora opened her mouth to say that yes, she'd come home because she needed a job, Cassiopeia waved her hand. "And it had nothing to do with that drama you'd fallen into. That was just an excuse. A crossroads, if you'd like. It was time for you to face your destiny, and fate obviously felt you needed a nudge to get you to do so."

"Right. Being under police suspicion, used by the man I was sleeping with and then fired from my job were all the work of fate," Pandora snipped.

"Of course not. Those were all the result of your choices, dear. Not bad or good choices, mind you. Simply ones you made without stopping to listen to your intuition. Fate just used them to move you along."

"Mom, stop," Pandora barked, perilously close to tears again. Was anyone on earth as frustrating as her mother? "I obviously have no intuition. So will you please let it go? I'm never going to be what you'd like. I wish you'd just accept that I'm a failure as an Easton so we can both relax."

Stepping back so fast her rust-and-hunter-green caftan caught on the corner of the counter, Cassiopeia gave a shocked gasp and slapped her hand over her heart. Even though her shoulders were tense with anger and her stomach was tight with stress, Pandora almost giggled. Nobody did the drama show quite like her momma.

"A failure? That's ridiculous," Cassiopeia snapped. She lifted her chin so her red curls swept over her shoulders, and crossed her arms over her chest in the same gesture Pandora herself used when she was upset. "Let's not confuse things here, young lady. You're not angry with me."

"No? Care to bet on that?"

"You're angry with yourself. And with good reason. You can't blame me for your choices, Pandora. Or for your inability to step up and accept responsibility for making them."

Pandora felt as if she'd just been punched in the gut and couldn't find her own breath. Yes, she'd made a mistake. But the mistake was that she'd trusted the wrong person. That she'd fallen in love with the idea of love, and overlooked the warning signs. Blinking tears away, she wanted to yell that she wasn't irresponsible. But her throat was too tight to get the words out.

"Until you trust yourself, you'll never see what's right in front of you," Cassiopeia said with a regal toss of her curls. "You're too busy being scared, running and doubting. And, sadly, placing blame instead of having faith in yourself."

"You have no idea what it's like," Pandora snapped. Fury was red, hazing her vision and letting truths fly that she'd spent most of her life hiding from. "I grew up in the shadow of your reputation."

"And you have a problem with my reputation?" Behind the haughtily raised brows and arch tone, Pandora heard a hint of hurt. But the words were already tumbling off her tongue and she couldn't quite figure out how to grab them back.

"I couldn't live up to your reputation, Mother. Nobody could. Especially not with everyone in town poking and judging me, and you always prodding me to find something that we both know damn well doesn't exist."

Cassiopeia sagged. As though someone had let the air out of her, her shoulders, face and chin drooped. She gave a huge sigh, then shook her head as if defeated.

"I can't do this again, Pandora. You refuse to hear me. You snub my guidance while hiding behind your insecurities." She swept a hand through her hair, leaving the curls a messy tangle around a face that suddenly looked older than her years. "Perhaps it's my fault. Not, as you seem to think, for being myself. I see nothing wrong with being the best I can and embracing my strengths. But I must have gone wrong somewhere if you're so afraid of life that you have to blame me."

Guilt was so bitter on Pandora's tongue she couldn't get

any words past it. Just as well, since she had no idea what
the words would be.

"I'm going home," her mother declared. "When you're
ready to talk…if you're ready to talk, I'll be there for you."

Pandora didn't know if she wanted to call her back, to try
to fix the mess they'd left splattered between them. Or if she
wanted a little time and distance, at least until she figured
out what she wanted to say.

But, as usual, it wasn't up to her. Her mother swept from
the room, taking all the choices with her.

"So WHAT'S THE DEAL? You're finally willing to talk? Or are
you just stopping by to check out the bikes?"

Hands shoved in the front pockets of his jeans, Caleb grimaced at his father's words. He looked around the showroom
of the bike shop, noting the gleaming chrome of the custom
hogs and a few Indians and shrugged. "They are pretty sweet-
looking bikes."

"Yeah, they are," Tobias agreed. He patted the diamond-
tucked leather of one seat and nodded. "Best game in town,
too. I get the parts dirt cheap, Lucas puts them together for
a song and I sell them at a profit of about one, one-fifty percent."

"Sounds like a legit business to me."

"I told you, son. I've gone straight."

"Why do I find that hard to believe?" He wanted to. He'd
spent most of his childhood wishing and hoping to hear his
dad say those words. Hell, the last thing he'd told his old man
before he'd left for college was that he wasn't coming home
until the guy was clean. But when Tobias had called two
years back with that same claim, Caleb hadn't bought it.

And now?

"There's plenty of challenge in making this place turn
a profit. Between figuring out how to lure in the gullible

and get them to open their wallets for a custom bike, special maintenance plans, yearly trade-ins and upgrades, I'm finding plenty to do."

"As challenging as scamming the head of a national bank out of five hundred large? How does customer service stack against selling bridge investments?" Caleb looked around the shop, noting that like everything his father owned, it was pristine, upscale and just a little edgy. "Does monthly inventory give you the same thrill as selling a fake Renoir to a reclusive art buff?"

Tobias's grin, so much like Caleb's own, flashed as he dropped onto a long, glittery red Naugahyde bench that spanned the center of the showroom. "Those were good times, I have to admit. But these are, too. The key to anything in life is to have fun with it, Caleb. If you're enjoying what you do, you'll live a happy, fulfilled life."

One of the pearls of wisdom Tobias had shared many a time with his children over the years. And frustratingly enough, the one that had been ricocheting around Caleb's head for the least year as he'd fought burnout and disenchantment.

"So tell me the truth, son. Why are you really here?"

"To see your shop." Caleb sidestepped. Then he shoved his hands into his pockets and sighed. Or to figure out who he really was, or some stupid touchy-feely thing like that.

Pulling his face in consideration, Tobias gave a slow nod. He got to his feet and walked over, patting Caleb on the shoulder before stepping around him and heading toward the back room.

Since that's the part of the shop Caleb really wanted to see, he followed.

The room was huge, with a mechanic's bench against one wall, toolboxes and an air compressor along another. He noted an open door leading to a bathroom.

"Here, have a cookie," Tobias invited, gesturing to a tray as he sat down at a small table. "The pretty little gal across the alley made them. Supposed to do wonders for your sex drive."

"I hear yours is doing wonders on its own. Isn't dating a woman your daughter's age something of a cliché?"

Tobias's grin was wide and wicked. He tilted his chair back, balancing on two spindle legs and considered the cookie in his hand as if he'd find the answer in one of the chocolate chips.

"Now, why are you really here? You're ready to quit that misguided cop job?"

Caleb realized that he didn't even feel surprise at Tobias's insight. The man was an expert. At reading people, at twisting situations, at understanding human nature. And as much as Caleb might have wished otherwise over the past thirty years, the old guy was his father.

"I think I'm done," he heard himself admit. Grimacing, he took a cookie. Maybe chewing would give him time to censor his mouth.

"I followed your career, son. You did yourself, and me, proud. Whatever you do next, I'm sure you'll be just as good."

Overcome with an emotion he couldn't quite identify, Caleb looked away. How odd was it that he'd just realized that no matter what his choices, no matter what he'd done in his life, his father had always believed in him.

He didn't know what the hell to do with that.

Before he could figure it out, something outside the small, barred window overlooking the alley caught his eye. Caleb ambled over, looking out just in time to watch two dirtbags exchange a fat wad of cash for several large pill bottles. He'd been right. This was the main drop spot. But why here?

"Do you have storage in the back?" he asked over his shoulder.

Tobias took his time selecting another cookie before he met Caleb's eyes. "Nope. But the pretty little gal does."

Son of a bitch. Pain, fury and disappointment all pounded through Caleb. Son of a freaking bitch.

How could it be Pandora? He felt like scum just thinking of her and drugs in the same thought. But this? They were using her storage unit, her store. Did she have a clue? Whether she did or not, this was going to be a major problem for her.

Caleb dropped his head against the window and closed his eyes, fury and despair ripping through him.

He'd reluctantly come home to clear his father's dubious name. But he didn't want to do it at the expense of the woman he loved.

11

CALEB CLICKED OPEN the file of mug shots Hunter had emailed. Impressed, despite himself, he had to admit the FBI had better toys than he'd had access to with the DEA. Within an hour of calling Hunter with a report of what he'd seen, a laptop had been delivered to his hotel, access codes had been texted to his cell phone and he'd had the files of eight guys who fit the description of both dudes he'd seen selling behind Pandora's store.

Throw in Russ, whose identity didn't match the info on his job application, and Caleb figured he'd nailed down the drug ring's middle-management team.

What he didn't have yet was the person calling the shots.

He took a drink of coffee, letting the flavor mingle with the rest of the bitterness he'd been tasting since he realized that the woman he was crazy for might be a criminal.

He'd been so sure she was clean. Just as he'd been sure Tobias was clean. He'd only dug into her computer files so he could tell Hunter that he'd done a thorough job.

Then he'd read the files Hunter had emailed detailing the illegal activities of her drug-dispensing ex and her part in his little prescription ring. And the note Hunter had attached warning Caleb not to do anything stupid.

What a pal.

Caleb considered pounding his head on the wall a few times, but figured he couldn't afford the possible loss of more brain cells.

Instead, he was going to ID the two guys, round them up and scare the crap out of them. Sooner or later, someone would spill a name. Or the boss would come looking for them.

Just as he started scrolling through the faces, there was a knock on his door.

He considered ignoring it. He wanted to ID this guy while the face was still fresh in his head. Then, he wanted to hit something—anything—hard, until it broke into a million pieces and left his knuckles bloody and raw.

But whoever was at the door might have another package from Hunter. And Caleb was definitely curious to see what other toys his old friend had to offer.

As a precaution, he closed the file, shut down the program and turned off the laptop. It was a secure machine, requiring two passwords, his own and the one Hunter had provided, to start it or pull it out of the hibernation it'd enter if left idle for more than thirty seconds. But still, it paid to be cautious.

He strode over and pulled the door open.

Well, well.

Not a toy from Hunter, but a toy all the same.

"Pandora," he greeted with a stiff smile.

For a brief second, he missed the old days when he'd opened the door to gun-toting, drugged-out, murdering dealers looking to take him out.

At least he knew what to do with them.

"Hey," she greeted with a shaky smile. Eyes narrowing, Caleb saw the strain on her face. Her makeup was all smudged and drippy, as if she'd been crying.

Yeah, a strung-out dude pointing a loaded .45 at his face would definitely be easier.

But not as important, he admitted to himself, heaving a heavy sigh.

"What's wrong?" he asked.

"Do you mind if I come in?"

Yes.

He stepped aside anyway.

And tortured himself by breathing deep as she walked past, inhaling her spicy fragrance and wishing he could bury his face in the curve of her neck and see if she tasted as good as she smelled.

Stupid.

Totally freaking stupid.

Because he knew damn well she tasted delicious.

"Are you okay?" he asked after a few seconds of indulging himself by staring at her as she wandered the room. She shouldn't be here. But he couldn't kick her out. Whatever her part in this, even if it wasn't purely innocent, he wanted— needed—this time with her.

"I'm…" She stopped by the window, giving him a pained look over her shoulder. "I had a blowup with my mother. Now I guess I'm confused."

"Parents have that effect," he observed. Finally giving in to the fact that running down the hall to avoid confronting her would be blatantly chickenshit, Caleb shut the door. He didn't cross the room, though. Instead, he leaned his hip against the dresser and watched.

"I know you're probably busy. You're not expecting me. But, well, I thought about going by Kathy's, but her family is in town and it'll be really crowded and loud there. And I just wanted to see if, you know, maybe…"

She trailed off, offering a wincing sort of shrug as she wandered the room nervously.

What was he going to do? Kick her out? Grill her when she was already upset? Yes, he knew that both were perfectly solid methods to deal with a potential drug-dealing mastermind. But, dammit, this was Pandora. And she was upset.

So he'd stay and comfort her. After all, he could be a chickenshit here in his room, too.

"What happened?"

"Confrontations and ugly words and painful truths," she confessed, trailing her fingers over the glossy knotty pine of one of the four posts of the large, quilt-covered bed.

"Sounds like a family reunion to me." Although he and his father had skipped over that part of reunioning. Instead, the old man had watched with laser-sharp eyes as Caleb had stepped to the side of the window so as not to be seen while the drug deal went down. Tobias hadn't said a word, though. He'd just arched one brow and given a jaunty salute when it was over and Caleb had said he had to go.

All that cordial silence had creeped him out.

"Not my family," Pandora said with a stiff smile. "Usually my mother is dramatic, I'm quiet and we both pretend everything is peachy keen."

She needed to talk. He could see it on her face, hear it in her tone. The previous night she'd needed sex, a little laughter and a chance to forget about everything else.

Caleb sighed, feeling the weight of the world pressing down on him all of a sudden. The sex was probably off-limits while she was a suspect, and the laughter was beyond him.

Dammit, that left talking.

He sucked at talking.

As Pandora poked a finger between the balcony curtains, closed against the night, he sighed again.

Fine.

"Want to have a seat?" he invited.

Her face brightening, she looked around. The choices were the bed or one of two club chairs next to the small table holding the laptop.

He really didn't want her near, either.

"I would, thanks," she said, taking a second to shrug off her thick white coat, laying it and her purse and scarf over one of the chairs. She hesitated, glancing at the bed, then back at his face. Then she squished into the chair alongside her coat.

Caleb walked over, picked up the laptop and moved it to the dresser, then sat across from her.

"So why's it a big deal that you tossed a few truths at your mother?"

"Because she tossed a few right back at me," she said with a wince.

He grinned for the first time in hours. "Don't you hate it when that happens?"

"I do. I had no idea the truth could be so painful. I think it was easier when she blithely pretended to go along with my claims that I was happy with my life."

"Pretending is never good."

"Sure, that's easy for you to say. You're confident enough to say screw you to everyone who doesn't accept you exactly as you are," she said with a rueful sort of laugh.

Cringing, Caleb's gaze shifted toward the door.

Was he? He didn't even know who he was, so how could he expect anyone to accept him at face value? For his entire adult life, hell, most of his life as a whole, he'd played a part.

"I admire that," she continued. She gave him a shy sort of smile and traced designs on her scarf with her finger. "I wish I were more like you. Only, not, you know. Because I really, really like being a girl with you."

He wasn't an expert on this talking thing, but he knew when someone was trying to sidestep to get out of delving into the deeper emotional stuff. And he shouldn't let her get away with it. She was hurting, and she probably should get it all out, talk and vent and spew and whatever the hell else women did to heal.

Miserably uncomfortable now, Caleb wished he'd paid more attention to Maya when she'd done this kind of thing growing up. That girl had always been talking.

"I guess you have a pretty good handle on your life, hmm?" she said, still sidestepping, though now poking her toes into his business. "You and your dad made up, you're free to come and go as you please. Or, you know, stay if you wanted."

Hey, now. Sidestepping was one thing. Poking into his life? Totally not cool. This was about her problems. Not his.

He leaned forward to tell her just that.

"We didn't make up," he heard himself saying, instead.

"But you went to the party?"

"Yeah."

"And didn't you hang out at his shop earlier?"

Caleb's eyes narrowed. Had she seen him while he was watching the drug deal go down? Was this a setup?

"He stopped by for lunch and mentioned what a great visit the two of you had," she continued, now watching her fingers poke through the scarf's fringe instead of meeting his eyes. "He was sweet. Teased me a little about the two of us, and said he liked me."

A hint of color warming her cheeks, she finally glanced up and gave Caleb a tiny smile. The kind that made him think of shy little girls sitting on Santa's lap, feeling like the most special princess in the world for those two minutes.

"He does like you," Caleb said absently, trying to figure out what Tobias was doing. That the old man was up to something was a no-brainer. But why did it involve Pandora? An inkling, a tiny germ of a hint, started poking at the back of

Caleb's brain. He couldn't see it clearly yet, but the same instincts that had saved him from multiple bullets told him it was there.

"He's a good guy," she said quietly. Then she wrinkled her nose and asked, "Am I not supposed to say that? I mean, if you guys didn't make up, you probably don't want to hear someone singing his praises, huh?"

"No," Caleb realized. "I don't mind. I mean, he's easy to like."

"He really is," she agreed, reaching over to brush her hand over his. He turned his fingers to capture hers, making her smile. "So is my mother. If you can get past her larger-than-life perfection."

"Is that a bad thing?" he asked, using a method straight out of Witness Grilling 101. Ask open-ended questions that kept the other person guessing as to what you wanted to hear. They were more likely to go with an unscripted gut response.

"Not totally bad. I mean, she's fun and always makes people laugh. She's got flare and talent and, well, she's just so exuberant and alive. She walks in a room and everyone automatically gravitates to her."

"So why are you so unhappy with her?"

She sighed, staring blankly across the room as she considered that question. He noticed that there was now an actual hole in the knitted scarf from her digging at the yarn.

"Because of all those same reasons." Her smile was a little shaky. "I mean, that's a lot to live up to, you know? She's larger than life. People all around the world know who she is. Then they look at me with this puzzled stare, like they are trying to figure out where she went wrong."

Caleb gave a shake of his head.

"What?" she asked.

"You just described me and my dad."

Her laugh was more a puff of air than amusement. She shook her head. "What are we supposed to do about it?"

He threw his hands in the air. "I don't know. I mean, they do a great job of being who they are."

"I think you do a great job of being who you are, too. So why is not being like them a problem? I don't know about you, but I'm tired of being measured by my mother."

Thin ice. Caleb hesitated before going with his gut. "But I think the only one measuring you by that is, well, you."

There went the sweet look off her face. She pulled back, her eyes narrowed and her lips tight. She looked as if she was seriously considering smacking him with that scarf.

"Me?" she asked in a tone so arch it was worthy of a queen.

"I guess I have an outsider's perspective," he mused. "I see a town that likes you, one that's actually a little defensive of you, if all the warnings I got not to hurt you are anything to go by. I see an intriguing, attractive woman trying her hand at something new and succeeding. A woman who loves cats, cooks like a dream and always has a smile and a warm word for people. Maybe you're not flamboyant and wild, like your mother. But you're just as interesting, and even more beautiful."

Her smile was bright enough to light the room. Caleb shifted uncomfortably in his chair, wanting to duck out until she stopped beaming at him. This gallant thing was more Gabriel's style than his. But he hadn't been able to stand seeing that dejected look on her face.

"So, I didn't bring any treats," Pandora said out of the blue, nibbling on her lip in a way that made him want to beg for a taste.

"Treats?"

"Yeah. Cookies or chocolate sauce or, well, you know. Aphrodisiacs." She shrugged again, knotting together the frayed pieces of yarn to repair her scarf. "I really didn't intend to come over. I was upset when I left the store and instead of walking home, my feet brought me here. To room seventeen."

Her words ended in a wistful tone he didn't understand. What he did understand was the look in her eyes. Sexy and appreciative. Warm and sweet. God, she was incredible.

Unable to resist, Caleb leaned forward and brushed his lips over hers. She tasted so freaking good. His tongue traced the full pillow of her lower lip, then he nipped lightly.

Her gasp was followed by a low moan of approval. She skimmed the tips of her fingers over his jaw, whisper-soft and so gentle. It was all he could do not to grab her by the waist and carry her over to the bed.

Caleb pulled away and jumped to his feet. Pacing, he shoved one hand through his hair.

What was he doing? She was the prime suspect in an FBI drug case. He should at least settle a few questions before he settled himself between her thighs.

"I can go," she said quietly, her hand dropping away from the buttons of her silk top.

It killed him to see that hurt on her face. To hear the self-protective distance in her tone.

It really all came down to faith.

He'd told Hunter he was sure his old man was innocent. But a part of him, the part that knew that there was a potential criminal in everyone, had wondered.

But Pandora? At the moment, all evidence pointed toward her. With what he'd seen, what he knew and what he'd heard, he'd have felt solid making an arrest.

But his instincts said otherwise. They said she was everything he'd ever wanted in a woman. Sweet and hot and adventurous. And, dammit, innocent.

So while he might be suffering from plenty of burnout and

his instincts were raw nerves at this point, he had to listen to them. Because without that, he was nothing.

He'd just have to prove the evidence wrong.

PANDORA WOKE THE NEXT morning with a feeling of absolute contentment. Eyes still closed, she stretched on the lavender-scented sheets and gave a deep sigh of satisfaction.

Yum. What a delicious night.

Shifting to the pillow next to her, she smiled and slowly opened her eyes. Caleb stared back at her, his gold eyes intense and, if she read him right, concerned. Why?

"Hi," she murmured, shifting back a little to get a better look at him. Stiff shoulders, jaw tight. He seemed distant, as if a part of him wasn't even here in bed with her.

Pandora shivered a little, then ran her tongue over her lower lip. What was going on?

But before she could ask, someone knocked on the door.

"Company?" she asked quietly, suddenly realizing she was naked except for the soft rays of morning light. She grabbed the sheet and quilt and pulled them higher.

"Probably Mrs. Mac with another delivery. Or muffins. She thinks I'm going to starve if I don't start each day with a half-dozen blueberry crumbles."

He sounded normal. But he still looked…fake.

"Hang on," he said, shifting out of bed and pulling on jeans, commando-style. He zipped them, but didn't bother with the snap.

Pandora's mouth watered. God, he was gorgeous. Sleek, tanned skin. That wolf tattoo crawling down his shoulder to growl from the gorgeous muscles of his upper arms. She wanted to nibble her way down the small of his back, then bite him. Right there on the butt.

Grinning to herself, she shifted to a more comfy position.

Starting the day with muffins and, hopefully, morning sex was a definite positive in her books.

"I could—"

"No," he said, shaking his head as he reached for the doorknob. "Wait there. I'll get rid of her. We need to talk."

She wasn't sure how scooting off to the bathroom for a very necessary morning function, to say nothing of hiding from whoever was on the other side of the door, would stand in the way of talking. But he sounded so weird that she didn't argue.

She watched Caleb peer through the door's peephole. He instantly pulled back and whispered something that sounded like a curse. Shoulders so tense his back looked like something in one of those men's muscle magazines, she heard him suck in a breath, then release it before opening the door.

He only opened it a few inches, though. With his body shielding her view, she could only surmise that it wasn't Mrs. Mac with muffins.

"Yeah?"

Her brows drew together at Caleb's impatient tone. Then she heard a man's voice. Deep, melodious and compelling.

"Party time," the voice said.

"You have the invitations already?"

Invitations? Party?

"All but the party planner. I'm counting on you for that."

Her frown deepened as she listened to the conversation. What the hell were they talking about?

"Let me in. We have to talk."

"Later."

"Now. Time's become an issue."

Caleb glanced over his shoulder at Pandora. The look in his eyes made her shiver just a little, it was so calculating. She felt bad for the guy on the other side of the door, since she was sure he was the reason for it.

"The hall?"

"Unsecure."

"You're a pain in the ass. You know that, right?" But Caleb stepped back and let the door swing open. "The balcony. Not a word."

Pandora gulped as the second man stepped through the door. Too stunned to be embarrassed, she just stared.

Holy cow.

Pure masculine intensity. He wasn't pretty, his face was too strong for that. But still, the sculpted features, long-lashed blue eyes and full lips did make quite a picture. His black hair swept off his forehead, longer in front and short in back. He stopped just inside the door when he saw her. Those vivid eyes cut over to Caleb and he arched a brow. Pandora tried to read his body language, but he was a blank. She didn't see even a hint of surprise on his part. Like walking into his friend's hotel room and finding a naked woman in bed was the norm.

The man gave Pandora a slight nod, his eyes doing a quick scan of the room, then he stepped over and opened the sliding door to the balcony.

"This might be a while," Caleb said, grabbing his sweatshirt off the footboard before following his friend to the balcony door.

"It's okay. I have to get to the store anyway," she told him with a warm smile. "I'll see you later, right?"

He gave her a long, intense look that made her stomach swoop into her toes. Then he nodded and stepped through, closing the curtain along with the door.

It wasn't until both men were on the other side of the glass with the door firmly closed that she realized Caleb hadn't introduced his friend.

Not that it mattered. She had her man.

And she missed him already.

Grinning at her own goofiness, Pandora tugged the sheet loose from the mattress to wrap it securely around her body, then slid from the bed. She padded over to the sliding glass door that led to the balcony and peered around the curtain.

Yep. Gorgeous and sexy. Both of them.

Giggling a little to herself, she did a mangled skip-step hindered by the sheet on her way to the bathroom.

Time to start her day. She had a feeling it was going to be an excellent one.

"TACKY, BLACK."

Caleb shrugged, tugging the gray fleece over his head in a useless attempt to ward off the morning chill. California or not, winter mornings were damn cold here in the mountains.

"What broke?" he prompted. He wanted the reason for Hunter's unexpected, and untimely, arrival. He did not want to discuss Pandora, his rotten choices, or what a jerk he was.

"I tugged a few more strings. Ran some numbers, looked at a few different accounts."

As if his toes weren't freezing, Caleb patiently waited.

"I know who the ringleader is," Hunter declared.

Caleb crossed his arms over his chest and arched one brow.

Hunter gave him a long look. Then, his fingers stuffed in the pockets of a very warm-looking overcoat, he nodded.

"You already know."

Even though it wasn't a question, Caleb answered anyway. "I'm pretty sure I do. Did you run the records I asked?"

"Yeah. All the names you provided had arrests that led back to the same person. Why didn't you email me with your suspicions?"

"I figured they might. These guys aren't local to Black Oak, so they had to have connected somewhere. Jail was the easy answer. I figured that'd be a good place for a clever drug dealer to recruit his team." Which was true. But it didn't answer Hunter's question. So Caleb admitted, "I didn't let you know because I don't know if he's working alone or not."

"You're worried about your girlfriend? I couldn't clear her."

Faint though it was, layered there beneath the official tone, Caleb could hear the regret in Hunter's voice. His old friend was hard-line about the law, but he didn't enjoy hurting people. Caleb flexed his shoulders and shook his head.

"It doesn't matter. Whatever you've got, it's bullshit. Because I know Pandora. She's not involved. Not knowingly."

Hunter didn't say a word. He just offered up that enigmatic stare of his. Caleb had lost a lot of poker money to that stare over the years. He wasn't losing Pandora.

"Just wait," he said, wincing, but unable to resist the cliché. "I'll prove it."

12

PANDORA WAS ALMOST skipping when she stepped into Moon-spun Dreams an hour later. A night of wild sex with a gorgeous man without any aphrodisiacal aid had done wonders for her attitude.

Well, that and the little pep talk from Caleb the night before had made her realize she needed to come to terms with her issues. After a night of sweet, sexy loving, she figured she was in just the right mood to try to make nice with her mother.

"Hi, Paulie," she said, bending down to rub her fingers over the silky black fur of the cat's purring head. "You having a good morning, too?"

"Hey, Pandora," Fifi greeted, coming out from the back room with an armful of fluffy handwoven blankets. "We can't keep enough of these on the sales floor. I'm blown away at how much demand there is for all this homemade, organic stuff you've brought in."

"I think it's a cyclic thing," Pandora said, straightening up and crossing over to give Bonnie's ears the same loving attention she'd offered Paulie. "Twenty years ago, holistic was all the rage. I'll bet in ten more, it'll be back to New Age glitz."

Something she'd do well to remember.

"Is my mother here?" she asked, heading back to the office to put away her purse.

"Um, no," Fifi said with a grimace.

"Something wrong?"

"I'm not sure. I mean, I know you're running the store now, but I'd thought that, you know, when Cassiopeia was back in town, she'd be involved. At least to do readings or something."

"Well, yeah," Pandora agreed slowly, turning to face her assistant. "Of course she will. That's what she does. We've had dozens of calls while she was gone, and people are going to be lining up to see her now that she's back. So what's the problem?"

"Well, you left right after your mother, so I didn't get to mention it. But I asked Cassiopeia on her way out if she wanted me to start booking readings. She said not until she found a place to do them." Fifi scrunched her nose, looking as if she might cry. "What's going on?"

Pandora shrugged a shoulder that was suddenly as heavy as lead. Like the fragile flame of a candle, her happy, upbeat morning disappeared into a puff of stress.

"What do I tell people?" Fifi prompted. "I've already had a few calls and I don't know what to say. Is she going to come back?"

Pandora almost said that Fifi should tell them to find a new psychic. Lying on the counter with her black-and-white face looking so patient, Bonnie caught her eye, making her wince. Besides being immature and spiteful, doing something like that would sink the store.

"I don't know," Pandora said, biting her bottom lip and trying to figure out how they were going to deal with this. "I guess she's upset about…" Pandora being an ungrateful brat who blamed her momma for her problems instead of pulling up her big-girl panties and facing them herself. "Something or other. I can call her later, see if we can get this fixed."

As soon as she said the words, the throbbing in her temples faded and her earlier euphoria returned. Yep, all she had to do was take charge and have a good attitude. No more hiding and running.

"I'm glad. I was telling Russ about the readings last night, how totally accurate they are." Fifi's grin made it clear that she'd been sharing a lot more than store gossip with the new guy. "He's a little scared to get one, but maybe after he sees how much people like them, he'll change his mind."

Pandora's gaze cut to her newest employee, who stood out like an awkward third wheel as he tried to help a customer choose between tumbled carnelian or a citrine spear. At least she supposed he was trying to help. It couldn't be easy with his hands hidden behind his back.

"Um, Fifi," she said with a grimace, nodding at Russ. "I know he's only been here a couple of days, but he's got to get past that skittish thing he's got going on."

Fifi scrunched her nose and gave a little sigh. "He's great with some of the customers. Younger ones, you know? He's bringing them in left and right. But with our regulars..." She winced as he held out a handkerchief to take the handful of stones the customer had chosen. "Maybe I told him too many stories about how powerful you and your mom are?"

"Sorry, what?" Pandora asked. The rest of the room faded as she stared at Fifi with wide eyes.

"Well, you know. You're the Easton women. Your gramma was a witch, right? And your mom is a famous psychic. You're so amazing with reading people, and then you made an even bigger splash with the café and all those aphrodisiacs. You always know just what to offer the customers, and how to keep them from getting all silly about it. Everyone talks about it. You're almost as big a legend now as Cassiopeia."

Fifi glanced at Russ, who'd rung up the crystal purchase and was now by the books with a young guy who looked as though he should be shopping in the herbal-bath section. "I'm betting Russ is a little freaked, you know? I mean, he's a believer, so it's all kinda intimidating."

Pandora couldn't care less about Russ anymore. She was too stunned by the rest of Fifi's words. She thought Pandora was on the same level as Cassiopeia? Fifi and the customers considered her one of the gifted Easton women?

It was like being enveloped in the biggest, brightest hug in the world. Pandora's heart swelled. Her smile spread from ear to ear and tears sparkled in her eyes.

"You okay?" Fifi asked, her own eyes huge with worry.

With a shaky sigh, she forced herself to focus and pull it together. There was nothing empowering about sniveling like a baby over validation.

"Sure. Yeah," Pandora sniffed. "I'll call Cassiopeia and get this fixed. Go ahead and start taking tentative bookings, letting people know that they might change depending on her schedule."

She glanced at the café and added, "Be sure to make the bookings for after two, when the café is closed. That way she has as much time and space as she needs."

Four hours later, the store was filled with week-before-Christmas shoppers. Both locals and out-of-towners browsed, compared and purchased enough throughout the morning that Pandora was ready to do a happy dance on the sales counter. She'd barely had time to leave her mom a message, let alone worry about how she'd patch things up.

By the end of lunch, her feet hurt, her cheeks were sore from grinning and she was sure they'd just had the best sales day in Moonspun's history.

She'd just pulled up the numbers on the cash register to check, when there was a loud furor at the door.

She glanced up, but couldn't see what was going on because of the throng of bodies. Then she caught a glimpse of red curls.

Showtime.

Cassiopeia took her time crossing the room. She spoke with everyone, stopping to offer hugs and exclamations to friends and strangers alike. With Paulie draped over her shoulder like a purring fur stole, and her flowing hunter-green dress and faux-holly jewelry, she was the epitome of famous-psychic-does-holiday casual.

Pandora leaned against the counter and watched the show. She didn't realize she was grinning until Russ stepped closer and whispered, "Who is she? She's famous, right?"

Her smile faded as she looked at Moonspun's newest employee. Fifi had said she'd known him, like, forever. And hadn't his application indicated he'd lived here for years? How could he have lived in Black Oak for *any* length of time and not know who Cassiopeia was? Heck, everyone in the five neighboring towns knew her by sight.

Before she could ask, though, her mother swept close enough to catch her eye.

"Russ, will you help Fifi cover the store?" Pandora quietly asked him. "My mother and I will be in the back. Please, don't interrupt unless it's an emergency."

His pale brown eyes were huge. The guy was a basket case. He was probably afraid they were going to concoct some magic potion or poke pins in a doll.

It was kinda cute, in a silly sort of way. She just patted his arm, then walked over to her mother. She heard him sputtering behind her as she went.

"Mom, do you have a minute?" she said, interrupting her chat with Mrs. Sellers. "I'd really appreciate it."

"Oh, here I am hogging your time and you must want to see your daughter," Mrs. Sellers said with a sweep of her hand. "You probably have so much to discuss. And you must be so proud of Pandora. She's definitely a chip off the old block. Or in this case, a crystal off the sparkling quartz."

Pandora glanced at her mother's face, expecting to see at least a hint of disdain. Instead, she saw just what Mrs. Sellers indicated. Pride.

Joy, as warm and gooey as her Hot Molten Love chocolate cake, filled her. Had her mother ever looked at her like that before? Or had she always, and Pandora had ignored it since it meant she'd have to move that chip off her shoulder?

"Mom, I'm so glad you're here. People have been asking about you all day." Pandora came around the counter and held out her hand. She put as much love and apology into that move as she could. "They're hoping you'll be available for readings soon."

Her mother's smile trembled a little in the corners and her eyes filled before she blinked thickly coated lashes and tilted her head in thanks.

"I'm glad to be here as well, darling." She rubbed a bejeweled hand over Pandora's shoulder, then spoke to the room at large. "I'm going to be spending some time catching up with my daughter. But I'd love to do readings. Fifi, will you go ahead and set up appointments?"

The perky blonde nodded. Before she'd pulled out a small spiral-bound notebook, there was a line of excited customers in front of her.

"You've brought in a stellar crowd, darling. Shall we go back and celebrate with cake or something sweet?" Cassiopeia said to Pandora, twining her fingers through her daughter's in a show of both pride and solidarity.

Pandora didn't trust her voice, so she offered a smile and a nod instead. Before they got more than two steps, though, the bells chimed on the front door again. Pandora's heart raced when she glanced over and saw it was Caleb. His sexy friend was with him, and the two of them made such a sight. Pure masculine beauty, with a razor-sharp edge.

"Can we talk a little later?" she murmured to her mother.

"I'm glad to see you have your priorities straight," Cassiopeia returned quietly.

Pandora glanced over, trying to see if her mother was being sarcastic. But her vivid green eyes were wide with appreciation. She gave Pandora an arch look and mimicked fanning herself, then tilted her head. "Go say hello, dear."

"Caleb," Pandora greeted, crossing the room. She knew at least twenty sets of eyes were locked on her, but she didn't care. Not anymore. She reached out and took his hand, then, determined to push her own comfort envelope, leaned in and brushed an only slightly shaky kiss over his cheek.

There. That'd show everyone. She was dating that bad, bad Black boy and she didn't care who knew. Or what they thought.

"Hello," she murmured. She was so caught up in her own internal convolutions that it took her a few seconds to notice his lack of a response. Chilled a little, she stepped back to get a good look at his face.

Closed. His eyes were distant and cold. There was something there, in the set of his shoulders, that carried a warning. As if he was about to tell her a loved one had died. But she glanced around, making sure her mother and the two cats were still there, all her loved ones were front and center.

Her gaze cut to Hunter, who looked even more closed and distant. Was Caleb leaving with him? Was that why he was here? To tell her goodbye?

Then he smiled and wrapped his arm around her shoulder. Confused, Pandora stiffened, trying to figure out what was going on. He didn't feel right.

"Sweetheart, I've been telling Hunter how great your cooking is. We stopped by so he could check it out."

She glanced at Hunter, dressed in jeans and a black sweater that should have been casual but wasn't. Yeah. He looked like a guy stopping by to sample cookies.

"Sure," she said, not having a clue what was happening. But it felt important, and secretive. So she'd wait until she had Caleb alone to ask. "Why don't you both come into the café. We have some pasta salad left, and sandwiches, of course. The cookies are fresh this morning and I have a wooable winterberry cobbler that's fabulous with vanilla-bean ice cream."

She babbled more menu options as she made her way through the curious onlookers, achingly aware of Caleb just a few inches behind her.

Once she and the two much-too-sexy-for-their-own-good men were in the café, though, she dropped the pretense.

"What's going on?" she asked, her gaze cutting from one to the other.

Their faces didn't calm her nerves at all. Instead, her stomach knotted and black spots danced in front of her eyes. Something bad was happening here.

"We have evidence that drugs are being run through your store. We want to use this space, today, to make the bust." The words were fast, clipped and brutal.

"Bust? Drugs?" Pandora's brain was reeling. "What? I don't understand."

Her knees weak, she grabbed on to a chair.

"Ms. Easton, there's a drug ring operating out of Black Oak. Caleb came to town to stop it. His investigation led to your store. We'd like your cooperation in apprehending the people behind the drugs, especially the ringleader."

She gaped. What the hell? Drugs? In her store? No. She'd changed the inventory, she knew every single item being sold here and unless saffron was now illegal, Moonspun Dreams was clean.

But before she could worry about that, she had to sift

through the fury pouring into her system like a tidal wave. Betrayal raced behind it, adding a layer of pain to her reaction.

"Wait," she demanded, holding up one hand. She arched a brow at Caleb. "You're a cop? You're not unemployed?"

"No. I'm not a cop and I am unemployed." He was, however, as distant as the moon right now. She noted his body language, how he was leaning away from her, rolling on the balls of his feet as if he was going to run at any second.

"Actually, you're on hiatus since your captain hasn't accepted your resignation," Hunter interrupted.

Pandora pressed her fingers to her forehead, hoping the pressure would help her sort it all out.

"I don't understand," she muttered. She took a deep breath and looked at Caleb again. She could see the regret in his eyes, as if he knew he was ripping her heart to shreds and was sorry. But he was going to continue to rip anyway.

"You think I had something to do with this? The drugs?" Her voice shook and she wanted to throw up. It was like déjà vu times a thousand. The humiliation, the pain, the heartache…

"Caleb has cleared you," Hunter said when Caleb stayed silent.

Cleared her. As in, he'd found proof against her guilt. Guilt that he must have believed in at some point.

"You thought I was involved? That's why you asked me all those questions before. Why you kept coming around the store? Why you—" Why he'd made love with her? Would he go that far? They did in the movies, why not in real life?

"I'll step out," Hunter murmured.

The gentle clacking of beads indicated he'd left. But Pandora's eyes were locked on Caleb's.

"You used me?" she whispered, her throat aching as she forced the words out. "You thought I was a criminal? Was everything a lie? Or did I just convince myself that what we'd shared was special?"

"No."

"No?" she repeated, her voice hitting a few of the higher octaves. "That's it? Just no? Care to elaborate a little?"

He frowned, shoving his hands into his pockets. As he did, his jacket shifted so she could see leather straps. He was wearing a gun. The room spun. Afraid she was going to collapse, Pandora reached out to grab a chair again.

"Look, it's like this—"

Before he could tell her what this was like, a rush of cold air swept over them. Then there was a quiet snick as someone shut the door to the alley.

Who the hell was using her back door? Pandora and Caleb looked at each other, her eyes wide with curiosity. His were filled with a cold warning that scared her just a little. His hand shifted to his hip.

She gulped, her heart racing as she tried to figure out when her cute café had turned into a nightmare.

Then she realized who it was and relaxed.

"Sheriff," she greeted, her voice shaking a little. *Way too much going on today,* she thought.

"Pandora. Black," the lawman greeted. He'd looked shocked when he'd first stepped through the door, but now his face smoothed into a smile. "Am I interrupting something?"

"No," she said.

"Yes," Caleb retorted at the same time. "But I'm glad you did. C'mon over. Let's talk."

Kendall's easy grin shifted as he studied Caleb's face. He took a single step backward, glancing toward the alley door. Pandora frowned, nervously gripping her fingers together. There was way too much tension in this room. She glanced at Caleb, trying to figure out why.

Whoa. She'd have stepped back, too. Caleb's smile was just this side of vicious.

"It's good to see you both," the sheriff said after clearing his throat. "I was doing my rounds, checked up the street and the alley and figured I'd come in. I hear Cassiopeia is back in town. Is she here? We've got a lot to catch up on."

His hand on the butt of his service revolver, he gave them a wide berth as he sauntered out of the room.

Pandora slammed her fists on her hips and turned to Caleb to demand an explanation.

"Quiet," Caleb ordered.

So she hissed back, "What the hell is going on?"

"Does he do that often?" Caleb asked, his words low and even.

"Sure, once in a while. Mother gave him a key for security and such."

The grim satisfaction on his face worried her. This was all happening too fast. Caleb being a—whatever he was—questionably employed in some form of law enforcement? Drugs, in her store. The sexy, intriguing man she'd fallen for and shared her body with now acting like something out of a crime novel. Too much!

"Let's go," he said, his large hand wrapping around hers.

"Go?" She dug in her heels. "No, I want to know what's going on. I'm not going anywhere until I do."

"C'mon," he said, gently but firmly moving her toward the beaded doorway with him.

When they reached it, though, he stopped and looked at her. His eyes softened and he gave a barely perceptible sigh. "Just trust me. Please."

With that, and a quick kiss brushed over the top of her head, he pulled her through the beads.

It was like walking onto the set of a crime show, with Hunter playing the part of the sexy agent in charge. He stood behind Russ, one hand on the younger man's back as he faced down Kendall. There were a dozen or more shoppers milling around, whispering and jockeying for the best viewing positions.

"Damn right I'm questioning your jurisdiction," the sheriff snapped. "What the hell do you think you're doing, coming into my town and trying to arrest one of my people?"

"What?" Pandora gasped. She was halfway across the room—whether she was going to Russ's rescue or to smack him, she didn't know—when Caleb grabbed her arm.

Confused and angry, she shot him a glare.

"What'd you find?" Caleb asked, ignoring her, the sheriff and the rest of the crowd to speak directly to Hunter.

"He had the key and the dope in his jacket pocket."

Caleb gave a sigh that probably only Pandora noted. Then he nodded and after giving Pandora a look that said *stay put,* he approached Russ. He stopped a couple feet from the young man.

"So let's hear it," Caleb said. "Who are you working with and what's this store's connection?"

This store? Working with? Oh, God. He really did think she was involved. And now the entire town would, too. Pandora felt woozy as the room spun again. Dope. Drugs. Déjà vu. She was so grateful when her mother hurried over and took her hand.

"You might as well confess. It'll go easier on you," Caleb promised.

Why was he doing this here in the store? Was he trying to ruin her? Pandora gulped as tears filled her eyes again.

Along with the rest of the crowd, she watched Caleb take a step closer. Hunter moved to the front door to block it. Russ shifted away, backing down along the sales counter as if he could escape through the cash register.

He bumped into Bonnie, who was sitting on the counter,

watching the show. She gave a low, throaty meow and butted him with her head.

"Git." Russ looked spooked, pushing the cat away.

But Bonnie meowed again, her head tilted to one side.

"What's she doing?" he muttered, a tinge of hysteria in his tone.

"She can read minds," Cassiopeia intoned melodiously.

"Nuh-uh." But Russ inched away from the black-and-white cat like he wasn't so sure.

"You might want to confess before she shares any of your secrets," Cassiopeia continued, sweeping her arm in an arc so the filmy fabric of her caftan flowed, wispy and ghostlike.

Bonnie meowed again.

Russ jumped. His gaze shot from person to person, locking for a long moment on the sheriff before he stepped closer to Caleb.

"I want a guarantee," he said, his voice shaking.

"Let's talk about this in my office," Kendall demanded. The guy looked totally stressed out and pissed, Pandora noted. His face was tense, and if she wasn't mistaken, that was fear in his eyes.

"We'll settle it here," Caleb said quietly. Pandora thought she saw an apology in the quick glance he threw her way, but then he was focused on Russ again. "Now."

"The guarantee?" Russ prodded.

His face impassive, Caleb walked across the room. Everyone held their breath, not sure what he was going to do to the young man. But he passed right by him and stopped next to the cat. Without taking his eyes off Russ, he swept his hand down Bonnie's head.

All eyes cut to Russ. The kid looked as if he was going to puke all over Pandora's imported astrology rug. He tugged at the hem of his T-shirt, his eyes nervously darting from Caleb to the sheriff.

"Who's your boss?" Caleb asked. "Your real boss."

Russ didn't even glance toward Pandora. Instead, he closed his eyes for a second, took a deep breath, then whispered, "Sheriff Kendall."

The chorus of gasps around the room was deafening.

Pandora pressed her hand against her stomach, afraid she might be the one to ruin the rug.

"Did he just accuse…?"

"He can't be saying that the sheriff…"

"Drugs? The sheriff? No…"

"I always knew he was shifty—"

"Enough," Caleb said. He didn't raise his voice or take his eyes off Russ, but the room immediately silenced.

"That's a major accusation."

"It's the truth."

"It's bullshit," Kendall said from the other side of the room. Furious, he looked as if he wanted to pull the gun from his hip and shoot someone. Tension expanded in the room like an overstretched rubber band, ready to snap at any second. Finally, thankfully, he slammed his arms over his chest instead, glaring at one and all.

Pandora met her mother's eyes, though, and tilted her head to indicate his stance. Shoulders rounded, chin low. He was lying. Her mother nodded in agreement.

"Who else?" Caleb asked quietly.

Pandora's heart raced. She glanced at Fifi, who had tears pouring down her face and had already chewed off three fingernails.

"Nobody. I mean, nobody I know."

She noted the set of his chin, the way his fingers were clenched together. She figured he was telling the truth. Her own shoulders relaxed.

"Why here? Why Moonspun Dreams?"

"I don't know. I mean, he, the sheriff, he said it was the

most convenient place. That with all the changes going on, the customers being a little weird and all, it'd fly under the radar."

Offended, the "weird" customers muttered among themselves.

"You used the storage out back. How did the store owner not catch on?"

Russ shot Pandora a guilty look, his face miserable and just a little green. "Um, well, I used to come in and hang out. I pretended I wanted to learn about all this stuff. Cards and magic and all that. I flirted a little, convinced Fifi that I could help out. That's it. The ladies, they didn't know anything."

"As far as he knows," the sheriff interjected smoothly. He'd gone from sounding pissed to looking like a lawyer trying to convince his jury. "But I've been watching this place for weeks. Pandora's made a name for herself selling more than just those sandwiches and cookies she's always pushing. Everyone on the street knows to come to her for their pills. Her reputation precedes her. Just check."

Pandora's outraged gasp was drowned out by her mother's furious roar. But neither of them had even inhaled again before Caleb moved. He strode over, and without a word or warning, plowed his fist into Kendall's face with a loud, bloody crack.

His hand grabbing his nose, the sheriff stumbled backward. He glanced, wild-eyed, at the crowd, then ran toward the beaded curtain leading to the café.

He didn't make it, though. As usual, Paulie had plopped himself in the doorway to sleep. Pandora didn't know if the cat sensed the drama, or if all the noise bothered him, but he jumped up on all fours and scurried between the sheriff's feet, sending the man flying into the far wall with another loud crack to his face.

Cheers rang out, but Caleb didn't smile as he strode over

and grabbed the guy, hauling him off the floor. He started reciting something, probably the Miranda Rights, but Pandora couldn't hear anything through the buzzing in her head.

She, along with what seemed to be half the town, watched the tall, dark and mysterious Hunter slap handcuffs on her newest employee while Caleb did the same to Sheriff Kendall. Her gut roiled with horror.

"Darling?"

She shook her head at her mother. She couldn't talk about it. Not now. Not here, in front of all the gawking eyes. It had been bad enough last time, when she'd come home to hide from her relationship with a failed criminal and everyone in town had whispered about her stupidity.

Now they were all here to watch, live and up close, as she confirmed it.

"Darling, come on. Let's go home. We'll have a nice pot of tea and some chocolate cake."

"No," Pandora said, sniffing as a single tear rolled down her cheek. She watched Caleb, one hand on the sheriff's back and the other on the gun holstered at his hip, stride out the door. He never looked back. "No. I don't think I ever want chocolate cake again."

13

"MORE TEA?" CASSIOPEIA asked, holding up her prized Hummel teapot she used for tea-leaf readings.

Her hands wrapped around her almost-empty cup, Pandora shook her head. "I should get back to the store. Or just go home."

Fifi had been a mess, blubbering and bawling as if she'd been the one arrested. Finally, calling it an executive decision, Cassiopeia had declared that the store be closed for the day.

"You need to go talk to Caleb, is what you need to do."

Pandora cringed, taking a sip instead of answering. The still-warm tea soothed her tear-ravaged throat. Then she stared into her cup, wishing she could find answers in the floating dregs.

"You've proven that you're a strong woman who knows what she wants and can make it happen," her mother continued, her voice both soothing and commanding. "Are you going to just let him go?"

"He lied to me. Worse, he made me look like a fool in front of everyone." Just remembering sent a hot flush of horrified embarrassment rushing through her. The whispers, the stares. It had been terrible.

"Dear, do you really think people care about that? They're so busy talking about Kendall that you're not even going to enter their heads. I'd imagine that's why Caleb played that scene out the way he did."

Pandora tore her eyes off her murky tea leaves to frown at her mother. "What do you mean?"

"He could have asked all those questions at the sheriff's office. Much easier, too, I'd imagine. He did that, made that big scene, just to make sure that people knew the drugs had nothing to do with you. That they had plenty of other things to talk about instead."

Pandora stared, first in shock, then in dawning hope. Her heart raced and she bit her lip. "Do you really think so?"

"What I think is that you need to go ask Caleb."

She was scared to. Pandora dropped her gaze back to her cup and took a shaky breath. She was afraid to hear that this had all been a scam on his part. That he'd used her.

Her mother gently laid her hand over hers and squeezed. "Darling, you have to face this. You can't move forward until you do."

"Is this why your clients all love you so much?" Pandora asked with a teary laugh. "Because you're so good at telling them what they need to do in a way that makes them feel great about themselves?"

"You mean because I'm a nice bully? Of course. Now listen to your mother and go get the answers you need."

Ten minutes later, her face washed and makeup reapplied, Pandora stood at the door of the sheriff's office. Her hand shook as she reached for the handle, so she pulled it back. Maybe she should wait. Come back later. Or better yet, take the week off from the store and wait to see what people really thought about the situation.

Then she realized that none of that mattered. All she cared about was what Caleb thought of her. So she took a deep breath of the cold night air and forced herself to grab the handle. Her knees were just as shaky as her hands, but she stepped through the entry.

Caleb wasn't there. She looked around the sterile, tan room, with its two desks and a few chairs scattered about. The walls and floor were bare, and the place smelled like burned microwave popcorn.

"Wow, Kendall is a sneaky liar *and* a lousy decorator," she muttered.

"Don't forget power abuser and drug pusher."

She jumped, her gaze flying across the room. Framed in the door leading to what she assumed must be the cells was Mr. Tall, Dark and Mysterious.

"Um, hi," she said to Hunter, shuffling nervously from her right foot to her left. "I came to see Caleb…?"

"He's finishing up the interrogation. He'll be out in a few minutes."

She nodded, then looked back at the door. Should she leave? She'd definitely rather, but something about Hunter's stare made it hard to run away.

She glanced back at him, then away again. Twining her trembling fingers together, she stared aimlessly around the ugly space.

"Would you like to sit?" Hunter asked, now leaning against the door frame in what she supposed was a casual pose. Except that he still looked as if he could kill a person with his pinkie.

"Um, no. I'll just… Um, maybe I should come back later?"

"Stay."

Command or request? Did it matter? Pandora bit her lip, then stepped farther into the room so she could set her purse on one of the desks.

"I've heard about your store. Intriguing. I didn't realize

your cat was psychic, too, though." His tone was conversational, but his blue eyes danced with laughter.

A giggle escaped, and with it, some of Pandora's tension. Who knew, superhottie had a sense of humor. It was hard to look at him for too long, though. He was so intense. If she wasn't in love with Caleb, she'd be stuttering and blushing and weaving all sorts of sexual fantasies.

"Bonnie's not psychic. She tilts her head because she had a series of ear infections when she was younger," Pandora replied, finally relaxing enough to lean against the desk. Then she paused, thinking back to both the cats' unnatural behavior toward Russ and Kendall. "I mean, as far as I know, she doesn't actually read minds."

His face impassive but his eyes still laughing, Hunter nodded and walked over to a small refrigerator and took out a bottle of water. He handed it to her with a small smile.

Wow. Maybe he wasn't that scary.

Pandora bit her lip, then unable to help herself, she blurted out, "What does Caleb do for you? He's…what? A cop? DEA agent? Why does everyone think he's an unemployed no-good drifter?"

"Because I am an unemployed, no-good drifter."

Pandora only jumped a little before turning to see Caleb standing in the doorway. Hunter just slanted his gaze toward the other man, then nodded and headed out the front door.

His hand on the knob, he turned back and told Pandora, "It was good to meet you. We'll talk again."

Her heart slamming against her chest, Pandora gave a jerky nod. She waited for the door to close before asking, "What's going on?"

"Russ Turnbaugh and Jeff Kendall are under federal arrest. We've commandeered the sheriff's holding cells until a team arrives to take them in."

"Federal?"

"Hunter's with the FBI."

"And you?"

"I was with the DEA, but I quit a while ago. Right now I'm exactly what I've said. Unemployed and clueless about what I'm going to do next." His words were as guarded as his expression. He looked as if he wasn't sure if she was there to talk or to beat the living hell out of him.

Pandora nodded, then looked away. A part of her wanted to beg him to make sure whatever it was, he did it with her. Another part, burned one too many times, warned her to hold back until she had the truth. All the truth.

"Are you working for the FBI, though?" Her chin high, she crossed her arms over her chest and tried to look in control, instead of on the verge of being a blubbering mess again.

"Hunter was my college roommate." He sounded less cold, more like himself now. She could actually see him starting to defrost. Whether it was because she wasn't hitting him, or he was shedding his interrogation-cop attitude, she wasn't sure. "We're friends. I was doing him a favor."

"I didn't realize the FBI looked into small-town drug problems."

"Not usually." He shrugged. "But there were extenuating circumstances in this case, and the drugs are a new blend. Something they wanted to stop before they gained a foothold."

"And you offered to help out of the goodness of your heart? Because you were bored being all unemployed and clueless?" Pandora winced, not sure where the anger was coming from.

"Don't blow this out of proportion. The bad guys are caught and they won't be using you or your store any longer. You're cleared and everyone knows it."

Cassiopeia was right. He had staged that little scene for her benefit. Pandora's heart pounded, emotions flying about so fast she didn't know if she should be thrilled, grateful or simply furious.

She settled on a combination of all three.

"Oh, no. No blowing things out of proportion. I should be relieved I won't have to go through weeks of grilling questions, false accusations and the loss of my computer and privacy this time." She was yelling by the last word. Apparently she'd glommed on to the fury more than all the other emotions.

Needing to get a handle on herself, Pandora held up both hands, took a deep breath. *Calm, center and collect yourself,* she chanted in her head.

Calm.

Centered.

Another breath, and she was pretty much collected.

"Look—" he said.

"No," she interrupted with a snap, whatever she'd collected scattering again. "I'm not finished. You came on to me. You poked through my computer, you made yourself at home in my house. You slept with me, over and over and over. And the whole time, you were investigating me?"

"I told you, you were cleared. I never suspected you, not really. Hell, you're not even the person I came to town to investigate." His jaw snapped shut. For the first time, Pandora saw Caleb angry. Not the stoic hard-ass thing he did so well, but really, truly angry.

Smoldering heat flared deep in her belly. It was kind of a turn-on.

"Look. You know the truth now. What's the big deal? Can't we just move forward from here?"

Move forward? Where? How? Wasn't this where he mounted his big black hog and rode off into the sunset?

The idea of that, of saying goodbye to him forever, was like a knife in her gut.

"The big deal is that I was falling for you and you were investigating me," she shouted. Horrified, she clapped both hands over her mouth. That was so not the way to dial back the drama.

CALEB FELT LIKE SHIT.

The rush of the bust, with its extra dollop of happy that he'd been able to take a schmuck like Kendall down, was gone. Now he was faced with the reality of what he'd done. With how he'd hurt Pandora.

"I didn't mean to hurt you," he said, knowing the words were totally inadequate, but having no idea what else to say. Pissed, he shoved his hands through his hair. He hated this. Hated not having a clue how to fix things with her.

"You lied to me," she said, her chin wobbling a little. *Oh, God, no. Please, don't let her cry.* Caleb wanted to grab her tight and kiss her until she forgot everything. Especially how he'd hurt her.

But he knew she wouldn't let him until he'd cleared up this mess.

"Not lied," he corrected scrupulously. "Just…withheld information."

"If not me, then who did you come to town to investigate?"

Caleb hesitated. Not only was it an open investigation, which meant the information was still confidential, but this was his father. Sure, the FBI had an entire database dedicated to cons they suspected him of. But most people, especially here in Black Oak, were clueless.

"Look, I'm not at liberty to divulge the details," he started to say. Her eyes chilled and her expression closed up.

"Because, what? You might lose your job? Oh, wait…"

"No. Because Hunter trusts me."

The ice in her eyes melted a little, but she still looked hurt.

Then she nodded. "Okay, I get that. It's not fair to ask you to break a confidence."

But it was fair of him to ask her to take him at face value? After everything she'd been through, unless he told her who it really was, she'd never believe it wasn't her. Caleb scrubbed his hands over his eyes, then blew out a breath. "Okay, you have to promise that this stays between us. You can't even tell those psychic cats of yours."

She nodded, a tiny smile playing over her lips.

"The FBI had tips that there is more going on than just the drugs. That someone with a lot of influence was using the town as their own crime ring."

She nodded, then gestured toward the door in the back that led to the jail cells.

"The sheriff, right?"

"Higher."

"The mayor?" she asked, sounding appalled. Then Pandora slapped both hands over her mouth and grimaced. "I'm sorry. I'm so sorry. I forgot she's your aunt. But, I mean, who is higher than the sheriff?"

Caleb gave her a steady look.

It didn't take her long. Her eyes widened and she shook her head in denial.

"Noooo," she breathed.

"Yeah."

"No way. I mean, I don't know what kind of evidence they have, but it's wrong. There's just no way."

"That's what I said."

"So you came home to prove your father's innocence?" she asked. Then her eyes rounded again. "And what? You had to prove mine, as well?"

"It's been an interesting month," he said with a laugh.

"No kidding," she agreed. "You must have been so worried. So scared of what you'd find."

Her brow creased in empathy, she took those two mile-long steps and gave him a hug.

And just like that, everything was okay.

Caleb's shoulders sagged as he returned her hug. He let out the breath he'd been holding and gave a half shrug. She understood. Totally got it. Instead of running disgusted from the room because his father was the kind of guy who triggered a major FBI investigation, she offered comfort and understanding.

He was so freaking in love with her, it was scary.

Tension and a fear he hadn't even realized was eating at his guts faded as Caleb tightened his arms around her, never wanting to let go.

Needing to taste her, desperate for more, he swept his hands down to the delicate curve of the small of her back, pressing her tight against him. Lifting her head from his shoulder, she arched a brow. Whether she was shocked or impressed by his burgeoning hard-on, he wasn't sure.

He took her mouth in a deep, desperate kiss. Tongue and lips slid together, tasting. She was warm and delicious. Everything he needed. Everything he wanted. Everything he hoped to keep, forever.

Then she kissed him back. Her lips moved against his in welcome, then in passion. Their tongues wrapped together in a familiar dance. Caleb groaned, feeling as if it'd been years since they'd been together instead of twenty-or-so hours.

They needed to get this all settled so he could have her again.

Gently, slowly, he pulled his mouth from hers. He couldn't stop touching her, though. His hands stroked up her back, down to her butt, then made the trip again. A part of him was worried that if he let go, she'd walk out and not come back. He had this one chance with her.

And he'd damn well better not blow it.

"So what now?" she asked, her hands loose around his waist as she stared up at him.

She probably wasn't referring to the investigation.

Time to put up or shut up. Nerves jumped in his stomach, but Caleb was ready for this.

"This is a pretty nice office," he noted dryly, looking around at the barren two-desk setup. "And now it's empty."

"I'm not doing it with you in here," she warned. "There's not enough Foreplay Chocolate Cake in the world to get me to, either."

He snorted a laugh. Grinning, he tucked a strand of hair behind her ear and pressed a kiss to her forehead. Had he ever been as happy as he was with her? Had he ever felt as good about himself as he did when he was with her? Was he ever going to find anyone who made him want to share himself, his life and his heart, the way he wanted to with Pandora?

The answer to all of those was no.

Still grinning, Caleb looked around the office again. Maybe it was time to stop bullshitting around.

"No, I didn't mean sex. At least," he corrected as he pulled her tighter between his thighs, "I didn't mean now or here. I meant…"

Pandora reached up to frame his face in both of her soft hands. Smiling, she arched a brow and asked, "Meant?"

"I meant, the position as sheriff will be open. I've got an in with the mayor, could probably snag an interim appointment until the next election."

Her eyes lit up and her smile was huge. Then she gave a little wince.

"What about Tobias?"

"He's not interested in the position. He runs the town just fine without all the crap that goes with an elected job."

She smirked. "No. I meant, can you live here, in the same town as your father? Does he know you were investigating

him? Will you be able to handle being his son *and* the sheriff in his town? That's a pretty big challenge."

A huge one. Because rather than clearing Tobias's name,
this bust had only pulled him deeper into things. Kendall
had claimed he answered to one person, and one person only.
Then he'd invoked the Fifth and refused to say another word.
Clearly, the first official job of the new sheriff would be to
find out who was trying to turn Black Oak into their own
little crime den.

But Caleb wasn't worried about handling the investigation. His old man was a lot of things, but he wasn't involved
in this mess.

"Can you live here, Caleb? In the same town as your dad?"

"When I was a kid I guess I thought I had to leave, get
as far away from him as I could so I could be myself. And
those are just about the most touchy-feely words I ever want
to say," he added, making her laugh. "But, really, he was
always there. He's a big part of who I am. He's shaped my
choices and my strengths. So living in the same town? That
just means he's talking to my face instead of being a nagging
voice in my head. As for the rest? It'll all work out fine. I
have faith that he's innocent in this, and I have faith that the
law will prove it."

And wasn't he all freaking grown-up and stuff. Caleb noticed the look in Pandora's eyes. Sweet acceptance mixed
with pride and just a tiny bit of lust.

Just as soon as someone showed up to watch the prison-
ers, he'd get her back to her place to do something about that
lust.

"You're really going to stay?"

He hesitated, then put it all on the line.

"Do you want me to?"

Caleb had faced a lot of scary shit in his life, but he'd never
been as nervous as he was at this very second.

And, dammit, Pandora wasn't making it any easier. Instead of wrapping her arms around him and declaring her undying love and gratitude that he'd be around, she pulled away.

She removed his hands from her waist, then leaned in to kiss his cheek before stepping back and around to the other side of the desk. What? She thought he'd get violent if she didn't declare her love?

He realized he'd clenched his now-empty fists and had to admit, she just might be right.

"This is hard for me," she said quietly, lacing and unlacing her fingers together. "I don't want to make a mistake."

Caleb's gut churned, but he kept his face clear. He was a big boy. He'd been shot at, called filthy names and once even been thrown from a helicopter—albeit a low-flying one. He could handle whatever she had to say.

"Don't try to sugarcoat things. Just say what you feel."

"What I feel? I love you," she said, the words coming out in a rush. Caleb grinned, barely holding back a fist pump. But apparently he didn't hide his triumph that well because she shook her head and held up one hand. "But..."

"No, let's skip the buts."

"But," she continued, smiling a little, "I've got a question. Or, more like a confession."

Caleb's triumph fled and his stomach went back to clenching. Shit.

"Are you sure you're not attracted to me because of the aphrodisiacs?" she asked, her words so whisper-soft he barely heard them. "I mean, every time we were together, they were involved."

"What? You're kidding, right?" She stared at him, big eyes filled with worry. "You're not kidding."

He moved to step around the desk, but she shook her head. "No, please. I get confused when you touch me. I need you over there while we talk."

Caleb cringed. Damn. He'd hoped a few kisses would suffice. Now he had to express what he felt with words?

"Pandora, I told you yesterday, you underestimate yourself. I'm crazy about you. I'd be crazy about you if we ate fast food, or if we ate nuts and berries, or if we keep eating all that delicious stuff you make. The food, that's just nutrition. Aphrodisiacs are all in the head, you said so yourself, remember?"

He cringed, knowing he wasn't good with the romantic speeches, but needing her to know how much he cared about her. How special she was.

"You're crazy about me?" she asked, looking at him through her lashes and smiling.

Needing to touch her for this confession, he took a chance and came around the desk. When she didn't order him back, he reached out for her hands, lifting them to his lips.

"I'm crazy about you," he confirmed. He looked into the hazel depths of her beautiful eyes and pressed little kisses to her knuckles. "I'm wild for you. I want you for you. You make me laugh, you make me feel good inside. You make me believe."

Her gasp was tiny, but he could feel her pulse racing as she bit her lip.

"I love you, Pandora. I really, seriously love you. And I want to give us a chance."

Her smile was brighter than the overhead lights. His heart filled with a joy he'd never imagined.

"I love you, too," she said softly. She shifted her hands so they framed his face, then stood on tiptoe to brush her mouth over his. "I really, seriously love you."

"And together," he promised, "the two of us are going to build a life. Our life, here, in Black Oak. I'm sure it'll have its irritants, given that our parents are always going to be larger than life. But it's going to be amazing, too. Love, laughter and a whole lot of that sexy chocolate cake."

"I have a large slice waiting back at my place," she admitted as she curled her fingers into his hair.

"With whipped cream? And hot-fudge sauce?"

Her smile flashed, as wickedly sweet as her cake.

"Always," she promised him right back.

* * * * *

PASSION

For a spicier, decidedly hotter read—
this is your destination for romance!

COMING NEXT MONTH
AVAILABLE DECEMBER 27, 2011

#657 THE PHOENIX
Men Out of Uniform
Rhonda Nelson

#658 BORN READY
Uniformly Hot!
Lori Wilde

#659 STRAIGHT TO THE HEART
Forbidden Fantasies
Samantha Hunter

#660 SEX, LIES AND MIDNIGHT
Undercover Operatives
Tawny Weber

#661 BORROWING A BACHELOR
All the Groom's Men
Karen Kendall

#662 THE PLAYER'S CLUB: SCOTT
The Player's Club
Cathy Yardley

REQUEST YOUR FREE BOOKS!
2 FREE NOVELS PLUS 2 FREE GIFTS!

⬧Harlequin® *Blaze*™

red-hot reads!

*Brittany Grayson survived a horrible ordeal at the hands
of a serial killer known as The Professional...
who's after her now?*

*Harlequin® Romantic Suspense presents a new installment
in Carla Cassidy's reader-favorite miniseries,*
LAWMEN OF BLACK ROCK.

Enjoy a sneak peek of
TOOL BELT DEFENDER.

*Available January 2012
from Harlequin® Romantic Suspense.*

"**B**rittany?" His voice was deep and pleasant and made
her realize she'd been staring at him openmouthed through
the screen door.

"Yes, I'm Brittany and you must be…" Her mind suddenly went blank.

"Alex. Alex Crawford, Chad's friend. You called him
about a deck?"

As she unlocked the screen, she realized she wasn't
quite ready yet to allow a stranger inside, especially a male
stranger.

"Yes, I did. It's nice to meet you, Alex. Let's walk around
back and I'll show you what I have in mind," she said. She
frowned as she realized there was no car in her driveway.
"Did you walk here?" she asked.

His eyes were a warm blue that stood out against his
tanned face and was complemented by his slightly shaggy
dark hair. "I live three doors up." He pointed up the street to
the Walker home that had been on the market for a while.

"How long have you lived there?"

"I moved in about six weeks ago," he replied as they

walked around the side of the house.

That explained why she didn't know the Walkers had moved out and Mr. Hard Body had moved in. Six weeks ago she'd still been living at her brother Benjamin's house trying to heal from the trauma she'd lived through.

As they reached the backyard she motioned toward the broken brick patio just outside the back door. "What I'd like is a wooden deck big enough to hold a barbecue pit and an umbrella table and, of course, lots of people."

He nodded and pulled a tape measure from his tool belt. "An outdoor entertainment area," he said.

"Exactly," she replied and watched as he began to walk the site. The last thing Brittany had wanted to think about over the past eight months of her life was men. But looking at Alex Crawford definitely gave her a slight flutter of pure feminine pleasure.

Will Brittany be able to heal in the arms of Alex,
her hotter-than-sin handyman...or will a second
psychopath silence her forever? Find out in
TOOL BELT DEFENDER
Available January 2012
from Harlequin® Romantic Suspense
wherever books are sold.